INCUBUS

J.D.Wheeldon

Indepently published through CreateSpace

First edition

Other works by J.D.Wheeldon:

Dark Fantasy

The Sanguine Lamb, Book 1 – The Blood Crazed Prince

CHAPTER 1

Everybody remembers their first time, whether it's a good experience or not. It sticks in your mind forever, it creeps up on you when you lie in bed at night or unexpectedly when you're absent mindedly sitting on the toilet. A memory that could haunt you forever, refusing to relinquish its mental grasp. I'll never forget mine, it's burned into my brain like a searing brand on the arse of a fat cow.

I was almost fourteen at the time, lay in bed in my leopard print shorts and a baggy T-shirt I'd had for years, the image of a colourful unicorn faded from the hundreds of times it had been through the wash. I lay with my leg thrust from under the covers exposed to the gentle breeze that blew against my sticky skin from the open window. It was late summer, the news said it had been the hottest day in twenty years and everybody had spent the weekend enjoying it, uncovering their pale flesh to the intense rays of the sun, blistering the skin like pink bubble wrap.

The scent of smoke still permeated the air from dozens of barbeques that were in full swing merely hours ago. The last of the drunken neighbours had stumbled home. Our house stank of sweet meats and alcohol from the garden party my parents had so graciously hosted, inviting the whole damn neighbourhood. It was strange how a brief stint of sunshine made the whole country so jovial, crawling from their dank caves to commune with those they would normally avoid, joining them in ritualistic feasts of glazed carcasses and carbonated alcoholic beverages. I guess it was a blessing really, England isn't exactly famous for its good weather and I had spent the day enjoying myself with friends and neighbours.

Regardless of the humid atmosphere and annoying chirping of noisy crickets, I had been sleeping soundly, until I suddenly awoke, my eyes jolting open for some unknown reason. Perhaps I had heard a noise, or perhaps my body subconsciously recognised that I was no longer alone. I rubbed the gritty sleep from my eyelids and sat up in my bed covers, damp with cold sweat. My hair was a veritable birds nest and my skin was clammy. I scanned the room as my eyes struggled to adjust to the darkness, lit only by the sickly orangeness of the buzzing street light outside.

My blurry gaze moved over to a shadowy corner of the room and that's when I noticed her. I froze instantly. In hindsight I guess I'm relieved that my first time was a woman, I've heard that men can be… rough, forceful, scary. She stood quietly, facing me and swaying as if inebriated. Thoughts raced through my head and I tried to make out her face, although this proved to be impossible as her long, dark hair covered it like a thick, black stage curtain. As she approached I could see the light reflecting off of her pale, naked body. Her skin was as smooth as porcelain, faultless and perfect as it stretched over her voluptuous curves. In a way she was simultaneously beautiful and terrifying.

My heart pounded through my chest and I pulled the covers up to my neck. I wanted to say something, anything but the words were trapped in the void of my throat, sealed behind clenched teeth. I wanted to ask who she was, what she was doing here, I didn't know if I should call for help but I was helpless to my bodies own fear. She reached the foot of my bed and my skin burst out into small pimples of goose bumps like the chicken thighs that had been roasting over a grill a few hours before. I was sweating but my temperature had plummeted along with the humid air around me. My breathing quickened when she moved on top of the covers, crawling towards me implacably as I pushed myself into the pillows, my legs squirming and my stomach writhing. I could feel her slender frame pushing against my trembling body as

I tried to convince myself to say something, to scream, to alert my parents of the intruder that was silently creeping upon me.

I opened my mouth but it was quickly covered by her fingers, her skin almost tasting strangely sweet in my mouth. My eyes filled with tears as she lifted her head. The shiny, black hair fell to the side, finally revealing her face. Dead, white eyes stared into mine like ceramic basins, lidless and cloudy. Her misshapen, yellow teeth clicked together as she ground them horizontally, jutting out from the pink flesh of her jaw like tombstones, drool hanging from them like cobwebs. The lipless maw opened and the foul, rotten breath whirled into my nostrils, bringing with it the acidic taste of vomit from my stomach.

I fought against her but with every thrash and kick her weight seemed to double. Her body pushed against my chest, forcing the air from my lungs. Her disgusting mouth flapped as though she were desperately trying to speak but the only sound that came was the hiss of rank air forced from her decayed lungs. Suddenly she froze, she became a statue and I stopped struggling. She began to lessen her weight and I gasped for air, my lungs free to once more fill themselves with precious oxygen. Her hand moved away from my mouth and she began to float upwards as if weightless. I lay motionless as her body hovered parallel to mine in the air above my bed. Salty tears welled in her pale eyes and fell, splashing against my face causing me to blink and flinch. When I opened my eyes again she had disappeared completely.

There was nothing above me except the stupid, pink lampshade I had chosen when I was ten. I cautiously sat myself up and looked around the room. Everything was as before, still and silent, undisturbed by the wraith that had appeared from the shadows. I leaned over to turn on my bedside lamp which filled the room in dim yellow light. Nothing. There was no trace of her. I touched my face and the only moisture I found was my own sweat, no tears, no putrid saliva. I threw the covers back to allow my skin to breath and my eyes grew wide in terror. My white bedsheets were stained red with blood, my blood. I felt sick and wanted to vomit. The woman hadn't injured me. I frantically moved my hands over myself, searching for a wound when I realised it was coming from between my legs. My friends had all come on before me, I was the last one, a late bloomer. We had learned about it in school a few years ago, but I hadn't imagined it to be this messy. Perfect timing.

I remained awake until the morning, questioning whether what I experienced was real, or whether it was nothing but a vivid dream brought on by my hormones. I considered myself to be a rational girl, but now I began to question whether I was losing my mind. I stripped my bedsheets, hastily stuffing them into the laundry basket, ashamed of the mess I had created. With a damp cloth I tried to remove the stain from my mattress but was only successful in smearing the blood deeper into the fabric.

The birds began to sing their sickeningly joyous tune outside and the sun peeked over the urban horizon and I ran to the bathroom. I was the first awake. I turned the shower on and stripped, jumping under the cool water which I expected to sizzle on my burning skin. I scrubbed myself with the raspberry shower gel that was my favourite, but would forever remind me of this horrific night, removing the dried blood from my thighs whilst tears contaminated the clean water. I sat under the shower, my knees brought up to my chest for what seemed like hours. Surely I couldn't have imagined the woman. She was so real, the sweet stench of her rotting face still lingering in my nostrils.

At the soonest possible moment I ran to my mum, tearful and sobbing, seeking solace in her loving embrace. I confessed to her about what had happened, babbling out the words incoherently, trying to explain in as much detail as I could remember so she wouldn't think I was a nutter. She did her best to comfort me, explaining that it was just a nightmare brought on by my first period and that it was normal. I knew she was lying. How could that be normal? None of my friends had ever mentioned experiencing anything of the like, although I knew I wouldn't tell them. I wouldn't tell anyone, I knew how crazy I sounded. But I also knew that was my first time, the first time I would encounter something paranormal, and I prayed it would be my last.

CHAPTER 2

The sun blazed down unrelentingly on the road ahead of us, causing it to ripple and melt like a mirage. I swear the summers get hotter every year, perhaps it was to do with global warming or something. All I know is that my back was stuck to the cheap, fake leather of Mum's car seat as I hung my arm out the window, snaking my hand through the wind as we sped down the country roads. The stench of manure invaded the car but it would be unbearably hot if we closed the windows. The air conditioning was broken in the greenhouse on wheels that was my mums fourteen year old Citroen.

"Don't look so worried," she said as she placed a sweaty hand on the skin of my leg. "It won't be so bad."

"Why can't I just stay with you?" I asked, obviously unimpressed by her plan to ditch me at her great aunts house in the middle of nowhere.

"Because you'll be safer away from me. Your dad can only follow one of us and he never even knew about my Great Aunty Wood's place."

I knew she was probably right, but it didn't mean I would admit it. Ever since dad went crazy last year, knocking me out and beating up Mum we had been on the run from him. Mum said the police wouldn't do anything because she had no evidence, but she said that he would take me away if he caught up with us. I found it hard to believe, Dad was always so kind when I was younger. He was always laughing and joking, him and Mum seemed so in love, we were the perfect family as sickening as it sounds. But I had never seen her so scared, and the bruises and blood on her face when I woke up in the car that night were evidence enough for me to convict Dad of the terrible deeds he had committed.

I stared out of the window, it was the only thing I could do. We had left in such a hurry that we had hardly any of our previous possessions and had to scrape by on what little money Mum was able to bring with her, emptying her bank accounts before Dad had any idea what she was up to. She loved me so much, but so did Dad. I tried not to think about him, the man who had forced us into hiding. Instead I occupied myself with watching the endless fields of yellow rapeseed that spread out as far as the eye could see. Like an ocean of sunshine that smelled like piss, did we really need to grow so much of it? Why couldn't these farmers plant some bloody carrots or cabbages or something more pleasing to the olfactory senses.

"So how come you never mentioned this great aunt to me before?" I asked, breaking the silence.

"Well I hadn't spoken to Aunty Woods since I was little," she replied, looking off into a distant memory. "My gran and her fell out when Aunty Woods wouldn't lend her some money to pay off grandads debt. She said he'd just piss it away again down the dogs. It's a shame really, I had some great summers around the estate, just like you will now." I had never heard her swear before.

"I doubt it," I said unenthusiastically. "I wish it would rain."

"Oh stop it, the weather's lovely!"

"Yeah, if I wanted to drown in my own boob sweat!"

We both laughed. One thing was for certain, since we had left our old lives behind, me and Mum had gotten a lot closer. I felt like Thelma and Louise, moving from town to town, always on the road. Except the towns of 1994 England were significantly less glamorous than they seemed in the States. As scary as the situation was, it was also a little fun. I got to skip school, we ate junk food, I stayed up late and Mum even let me drink alcohol, from time to time. Perhaps that was all just to mask the fact that our family had been torn apart. My childhood was happy and I was now living a life that was completely alien to me and just as I was getting used to it, I would be dumped in a dusty old stately home in the arse end of nowhere.

"So what's this place like?" I asked, eager to get more information before I was abandoned.

"To be honest I can't remember that much of the house, other than it was big. Very big."

"Is there a pool?"

"Erm, no, I don't think so," she said absently.

"I thought you said you had a lot of good memories of this place."

"I do, but it was a long time ago Bea."

"Alright alright, so what's Aunty Woods like?"

"Oh she's very old now, you probably won't see much of her to be honest. But don't worry, Tobias and the rest of the staff will look after you."

"Tobias?!" I scoffed. "What kind of name is that? He sounds like a right toff."

"He's sort of in charge, you do as he tells you. I've already spoken to him and let him know you'll be staying for a while. Try not to be too much trouble, it's a big place and there's not a lot of people around to look after it."

"Me? Trouble?" I joked.

She smiled at me caringly before turning her attention back to the road. We had been driving all day, through quaint villages and lush farmlands. I had never seen such empty roads before and it was almost peaceful. I saw a signpost coming up in the distance by the side of a dirt road. I pulled my aviator sunglasses from the top of my head back over my eyes, shielding them from the harsh rays of the sun, making it easier for me to read the faded words on the sign. *Berrington Farm.* The sign looked old and worn, just like the road next to it which curved off behind a row of tall trees, obscuring the farm buildings from view.

"Does anybody actually live out here apart from your great aunt?" I asked, realising how cut off from modern civilization I actually was.

"Not really," came the expected reply. "Just a few farmers but that's about it."

"Brilliant."

"It'll do you good to get some country air anyway. Now keep an eye out, we're almost there."

I loudly exhaled and thrust my hand back out into the breeze, desperate for any way to cool myself. As we drove on for a few more minutes I noticed the land start to change. The fields became much less yellow and wooded areas became more common. Thick tangles of hedgerows lined the roads, their crisp leaves dead from the lack of moisture and intense heat. The car became instantly cooler as we drove through the trees of the thick woodland which blanketed us with their shade. I looked all around but could barely see anything through the thick undergrowth of gnarled branches and thorny bushes. The road was ill kept, littered with rotten branches and dried, fallen leaves which made the car rumble and bounce as we sped along.

Eventually we drove through a pair of tall, rusted metal gates, entangled in withered ivy that snaked and strangled the iron bars, assimilating them into the undergrowth of the woods themselves. The road curved around a sharp corner and the house came into view as the trees began to thin. She wasn't kidding when she said it was big. It was fucking huge.

"Jesus! Why didn't you tell me we were rich?" I exclaimed in awe of the huge manor house we were pulling up to.

"We're not rich Bea, far from it. This big old house costs a lot to take care of, but all in all its not actually worth that much," Mum said, her tone quite low and sad as though the thought deeply upset her.

The road turned to gravel which crunched underneath the car tires and we pulled up outside the entrance in a cloud of grey dust. The house was a gigantic square block, three or four storeys tall like with cruel, spiked railings lining the flat roof like an intimidating, gothic prison. The rendering had crumbled away in patches revealing the brickwork underneath and the tall, thin windows looked down upon us like staring eyes, hiding the cavernous darkness of the house behind them. The entrance lay at the top of several stone steps and consisted of two monolithic, castle-like wooden doors, painted what once would have been a bright red, but was now faded and peeling and were already open when we arrived, mockingly inviting and imposing.

A tall, smug man was stood waiting for us, stood in the shade of the alcove wearing a dark, plain suit with a crisp white shirt. His hair was dark and thick, sloppily combed to the side in an attempt to look smart and sophisticated. He was closely shaved and had piercingly dark eyes, set deep into his pale face. He bore the look of someone cruel and full of contempt, standing proud and straight, looking down on the rusted french vehicle that had the audacity to park at the entrance to this great structure.

Mum got out first while I waited behind, I already felt like I didn't like this guy and was in no rush to meet him.

He shouted confidently with his hands behind his back. "Judith and Beatrice I presume."

"Yes," acknowledge mum. "You must be Tobias."

"Quite right mam," He said pleasantly enough as he began to descend the grey steps towards the car. "Please, allow me to help you with your luggage."

"Don't bother," I said defiantly as I slammed the passengers side door closed, dragging the small suitcase which carried my meagre possessions behind me. "I've not got a lot."

"Indeed," he said, looking down at me like something he'd scraped off of the bottom of his highly polished shoe.

"Tobias, could I ask where my aunt is?" Asked Mum. I had never seen her put in so much effort to be polite and courteous. I don't know why she felt the need to impress him.

"I'm afraid to say Mrs Woods is rather under the weather at the moment," came the reply as if rehearsed. "She seems to have come down with something of the flu and does send her apologise.

She will be down to greet young Miss Hammond when her strength returns."

"Oh dear, I hope it's nothing serious," said Mum, genuinely concerned.

"Worry not, I assure you it is quite mild. She should be back to her usual self in no time at all. Now, shall we go inside."

"I'm afraid I can't hang around, I have to be back in Blackawton by tomorrow to meet with the police."

"You're not staying the night?!" I asked shocked by Mum's response, my anger quickly replaced with worry and concern. I didn't think she'd be leaving so quickly. I knew it was silly of me, and I was seventeen, but the thought of being left alone in an old mansion with people I didn't know left me feeling uneasy.

"I can't Bea, I already made plans to meet with the detective and it took us longer to get here than I thought. Don't worry though, you'll be fine. Tobias will be looking out for you for now."

"I assure you Miss, you have nothing to fear here."

Mum walked over to me and hugged me tightly. I stupidly felt tears begin to swell in the corner of my eyes and fought them back, blinking them away. I was being ridiculous.

"It won't be long Bea, a week or two tops," she reassured. "You'll be safe here. Don't forget that I love you. I'll call when I can."

I wiped my eyes, hoping she hadn't noticed the tears.

"Yeah sure, I love you too. Try not to be late. This place gives me the creeps."

She smiled and got back in the car. A cloud of black soot kicked out of the exhaust as the decrepit engine erupted into life. She waved as she drove off, flashing an upset smile. She probably felt as crappy as I did but did a better job at hiding it. As the car trundled out of view I turned around and looked up at the bony face of Tobias, picking up my suitcase from the dusty ground.

"Right, lead the way Jeeves."

CHAPTER 3

I opened my eyes and looked down towards the end of the corridor. I had no idea where I was. The hallway was long and thin, exerting a feeling of claustrophobia on me, a fear I didn't know I had until now. It was dimly lit and smelled damp and dusty like a leaky attic after a heavy storm. Where the fuck was I? I started walking forwards, the old wooden floorboards creaking beneath the weight of my bare feet. Wherever I was it was old, the duck egg wallpaper was bleached and peeling from the walls. Empty picture frames hung at crooked angles and light fixtures had fallen to the floor, now covered in a thick layer of dust, the bulbs shattered into sand and blown away long ago.

As I veered around the corner I walked out into a large hallway. The great, tall windows had been boarded up, barring any natural light from entering into the building. I walked towards the edge of the gallery, hoping to look down to the floor below but thought better of it as the floor moaned intensely beneath me. I didn't know how high I was, a fall could be dangerous. The dim light made it difficult to see further than five or six feet and I opened my eyes wide to try and absorb as much light as possible. How was I going to get out of here? I didn't even know where I was supposed to be or what I was supposed to be doing.

Without warning I felt a cool breeze caress the nape of my neck as though a window somewhere had been opened to allow these foetid rooms to breath. I turned to try and evaluate where the wind was coming from and as I did I could swear I heard a voice from the direction I was originally facing. Spinning on my heels I scoured the darkness to find any signs of life but met with only unending darkness once again.

"Beatrice."

The voice, it called my name. Quietly, no more than a whisper, but as clear as a bellowing roar in the creaking silence of my mysterious surroundings. I tentatively stepped forwards, making as little sound as possible on the threadbare carpet.

"Beatrice, this way."

Again it called to me. The hairs stood up on my arms and a chill ran down my spine. I froze. Who was this person? The voice was definitely female, was she trying to help me? Or perhaps she was luring me to my death. Either way I didn't have much choice. I didn't know how else I would escape this bizarre maze or what lay waiting in the darkness for me to stumble upon. I headed for the corridor entrance I thought the voice came from, fearful but strangely curious.

As I peered around the corner I could see the corridor lit at one end by dim, yellow filament bulbs attached to floral lamps on the walls. A dark, feminine figure stood at the end and darted away as soon as my vision focused on her.

"Wait!" I shouted, setting off, not caring to keep quiet any longer. Was I crazy? Chasing a stranger through the darkness isn't something I'd normally find myself doing. I picked up the pace and followed the hallway around, striding past closed doors and broken furniture. I almost missed a narrow side corridor to my left when I heard the meek voice call out again, catching my attention.

"Here."

I turned and proceeded forwards. In front of me was a steep, wooden staircase. As I approached I could see it ascending upwards to the next level, perhaps an attic room. The top of the stair was brightly lit from a naked lightbulb that buzzed incessantly, suspended above a bright red door. The door was so saturated that it almost hurt my eyes, it was a stark contrast to the dull greys and browns of the rest of the environment and seemed brand new or freshly painted. Did the voice want me to go up?

As I began to ascend the stairs I felt an unusual feeling in my stomach. Much more than fear or nervousness, my intestines felt as though they were alive, writhing around like a ball of snakes seeking an exit. I began to feel nauseous and my mouth filled with drool. I held on to the rough bannister and tried to steady myself, concentrating on not throwing up.

"Beatrice."

The voice again, only this time it was behind me. Right behind me. I could hear the ragged breaths of whoever was to my rear, the warm air blowing on the back of my neck. I turned slowly, not knowing what to expect. Stood before me was a woman, or what used to be a woman. She stood naked, her pale skin hanging from her boney form like a skeleton wrapped in white leather. Her damp, think, black hair hung raggedly from her head, matted in a dark brown, congealed liquid. Her eye sockets were empty, each a black void that stared back at me, looking vacantly through me as her hunched body swayed in the harsh light of the electric bulb.

I stumbled backwards, reaching for the bannister but missing entirely, landing on the step behind me with a thud. The female corpse staggered forwards, her bony fingers reaching towards me as her jaw hung limply open, propelled by impossibly thin limbs.

"No! Get away!" I screamed in terror as I desperately scrambled backwards and upwards. My extremities were like jelly, the strength drained from them and I was unable to move effectively. The creature grasped my shirt and pulled me towards her with strength that belied her scrawny limbs. She opened her mouth and her rank breath assaulted my olfactory senses, once again bringing vomit dangerously close to my mouth. She uttered one, long word as she held me close.

"Run."

*

My eyes shot open and I lurched up, greedily consuming the air of the musty bedroom as I struggled to control my rapid breathing. Clutching at my t shirt, damp from sweat, I quickly scanned the unfamiliar room and remembered where I was. Fuck, I was dreaming. It felt so real, so tangible. That gruesome, haggard corpse of a woman almost seemed familiar to me, had I seen her before? I tried to put it out of my mind and shuffled back down under the light duvet. The wind blew outside and the untamed shrubbery and trees cast eerie shadows against the faded wallpaper of the grand bedroom I had been allocated.

This was brilliant, not only had I been forced to stay in this horrid house, but I was now having nightmares, I hadn't had nightmares in years, it would usually take nothing less than a blaring train horn to wake me. I couldn't shut my mind off, the red door kept replaying across my vision. For some reason the mystery of what was behind there had attached itself to my thoughts and would not relinquish any peace. I may have dozed off one or two times but the rest of the night was mostly spent tossing and turning. Between the horrid dreams and the hot weather there was practically zero chance of getting slapped by the sandman again and I was left awake with nothing but my own troubled thoughts keeping me company.

I lay there for hours, semi sleeping, not noticing the sun rising or the morning chorus beginning its recital and was rudely interrupted by a sharp rapping on my bedroom door.

"Miss Hammond?" Enquired a meek voice from the other side. She was so quiet I could hardly hear her and panicked as I feared the despicable creature from my nightmares had come calling yet again.

"Yeah?" I said groggily, unaware if I was replying to anyone at all other than my strange imagination.

"It's Miss Meadwell love, the housemaid. Tobias has told me to let you know breakfast is on the table. He said it wouldn't be there for much longer so if you were hungry it's probably best you pop downstairs Miss." She said politely. I had the sense that she wasn't really used to talking to people, never mind about giving them orders but I was intensely relieved that the voice came from someone real, someone alive.

"Oh, okay. I'll be down in a minute." I replied, rubbing the sticky sleep from my eyes. I was hungry. Normally I would skip breakfast, but being up most of the night had tired my body and it demanded fuel.

I threw on some old skinny jeans and a baggy t shirt that didn't smell of sweat and petrol. Throwing my hair into a messy bun I opened the old wooden door, which creaked on its hinges, and made my way down the corridor into the grand entrance hall which must have served as fuel for my overactive imagination in the previous nights dream. The room was huge and well lit, probably the best kept room in the house. An enourmous, bronze chandelier hung from the ceiling between twin staircases leading up to the first floor gallery. It was covered in cobwebs, so much so that it looked like a delicate, silk net had been draped over it. Nevertheless it was still impressive.

I descended the stairs in twos, my red Converse Allstars squeaking against the hardwood steps and making a thud as I landed on the parquet floor of the hall. I wasn't familiar with the layout of the house, Tobias had given me a brief informative talk which I had pretty much ignored, but I could smell my way to the food. The heavenly, salty scent of bacon fluttered down a corridor to my left and my nostrils practically dragged me in that direction.

I entered a largeish kitchen, occupied by a slender woman in her late twenties who was hard at work wiping the surfaces. She wore a simple black, knee length dress with a white apron. It was buttoned up tightly to a collar which framed her delicate neck. Her face was very plain with sharp eyes, a pointed nose and red lipstick that she must have applied in the dark. I could have done better with my feet. Her hair was tied in a simple ponytail and was dark and straight. She noticed me walk through the door and smiled nervously.

"Oh that was quick!" She exclaimed with surprise. I recognised the voice as the mouse like one that had informed my of the morning meal. “Please, take a seat at the table over there. Would you like a drink? Tea? Coffee?”

“Yeah coffee, black,” I grunted. I was not a morning person.

“Right away. I’m Miss Meadwell by the way,” she said with a big grin.

“Yeah I know,” I said, rather rudely i guess. I couldn’t deal with people who were so chirpy in the morning. What gives them that right? “I’m Bea.” I sat down at the table and opened the new loaf of bread that lay in the centre beside the freshly cooked bacon, sausages and eggs.

“Oh yes I know dear, we were all informed that you would be staying here,” she said as she busied herself opening a new jar of Carte Noire with the satisfying pop of foil. I buttered two slices of stale bread and slopped on some of the bacon, not as crispy as I usually like it.

“How many people live, er, or work here?” I asked.

“Well there’s me, Tobias, he’s in charge.”

I nodded.

“Then Mr Imamu, he tends the grounds and gardens. Of course Mrs Woods herself and then Jonah materialises from time to time, but he cannot… doesn’t stay with us.”

“Jonah?” I asked, but interrupted as the tall, well dressed figure of Tobias marched into the room.

“Less of the chit chat Miss Meadwell, there’s plenty of work to be done,” he snapped, walking over and taking the coffee from her. She looked away, her facial expression quickly shifting to one of concern, like a child caught in the act of scrawling up a newly painted wall.

"Of course sir," she said in the meek voice once again. "I was just about to pop upstairs to gather Miss Hammond's dirty clothes."

"Well, off you go then," he said sharply as she trotted off, her small heels clopping against the yellow stained floor tiles. Tobias walked over and plonked the cup of coffee in front of me as I stuffed my face with the bacon butty I had hastily prepared, avoiding eye contact with him. I could feel him staring, burning down on me. It was so uncomfortable I had to look up.

"You look terrible, did you not sleep well?" He snidely asked.

"No, it was too hot," I lied.

"You'll get used to it. Perhaps you should venture outside, breath in the fresh air. It will do you some good to get that filthy, city stink from out of your lungs."

I smiled sarcastically, revealing the chewed up bread in between my teeth and he curled his face up in disgust. I didn't like him, I could tell we were going to bash heads eventually.

"Listen to me," he commanded in a low, deep voice. "I've got plenty to do around here without having to babysit an overconfident brat. Stay out of trouble and you might even enjoy your stay. Don't touch anything, don't go anywhere and don't do anything without *my* permission. Clear?"

"Crystal," I answered, drowning in sarcasm as he rolled his eyes.

"Clean your plate when you've finished. Miss Meadwell will take care of the rest." He turned swiftly and made his way off into the dark recesses of the mansion, no doubt busying himself with menial tasks. If there was so much work to do why was the house such a shit hole? There seemed to be dust and cobwebs everywhere, only the busiest rooms and corridors seemed clean, and shoddily cleaned at that. Otherwise you wouldn't be reprimanded for thinking the house hadn't been lived in for twenty years. Something seemed off in the way Tobias threw his weight around and Miss Meadwell almost seemed scared of him. I didn't trust him at all, but he wouldn't have been the first man in my life to lose my trust.

CHAPTER 4

As much of a knob Tobias was, he was also right. It would probably do me good to go out and explore the estate grounds, I felt so clammy and groggy from the previous night and the house felt like a greenhouse with condensation collecting on its rank, cloudy windows. I could hardly stand the old stench in the air and needed to breath in something fresher. I ran upstairs, washed my face and threw on some denim shorts, the only thing cool I had left after Miss Meadwell had raided my room, seemingly taking all of my clothes to wash. She'd better not mix the colours.

I plodded down the stairs back into the entrance hall and through the heavy wooden doors out into the open world. Jesus, the sun was bright, piercing through the thin wisps of cloud to burst my retinas. I pulled on my sunglasses and gave myself time to adjust to the light. I walked forwards and onto the gravel, turning to look at the house again. If it weren't in such a state of disrepair it would be such an impressive building, full of elegance and grandeur. I imagined it once held luxurious dinner parties to wealthy families from all around, the family who owned it would be held in the most highest esteem. Now it only entertains the spiders and rats in their mockery of life and egregious consumption of it. I prayed to God there weren't actually any rats in there, but who was I kidding. It practically screamed rat orgy.

I plodded off and around the corner, interested to see the state of the gardens. Thickets of thorny rose bushes, dead from the heat lined the front and transformed into an amalgamation of other plants the further around the house I walked. Their dried, spindly limbs seemed to reach out in search of a drop of water that would forever be denied to them, frozen in death. Some were still alive, but they mainly consisted hardy weeds that smelled like urine or sweet, sickly garbage.

I noticed somebody knelt down by one of the dried up flower beds, trowelling and digging through the dust in an attempt to remove the weeds and detritus from the nutritionless soil. He was hunched over and seemed rather heavy set. He wore a boring set of beige overalls, dirty with mud and grass stains. His skin was dark and his white hair stuck out from underneath a baseball cap. He turned to look at me as I approached and nodded, causing me to quickly change my direction.

Great way to make yourself look like a massive racist I thought to myself. *First time you meet him and you obviously avoid walking near him.* I tried to convince myself otherwise. I'm sure anyone would do the same thing when they meet someone they don't know and aren't in the mood for idle chit chat. I Should go and speak to him, but would that make it more obvious? This is stupid. I'm not racist, and I don't need to prove it. Whatever.

Before I knew it I had wandered close to a wooded area a little way from the house. The thick wall of trees blocked out a large portion of the sun's burning rays and the cool shade felt like a wet towel draped over my scorched, pale skin. It was heaven. The earthy scent of peat and moss filled my nose and the eerie slits of light danced over the tall, up reaching shrubbery that grew at the edge of the trees. I sat down in the shade and ran my fingers through the soft, hair like grass, the morning dew wetting my fingers.

I sat and gathered my thoughts when it occurred to me how weird this place was. The people who worked here seemed constantly busy, tending to the house and grounds around it. But everything was in such a state of ruin and neglect that it begged the question what had they been doing up until now? Perhaps they didn't work normally. Perhaps they were lazy freeloaders, taking my great aunts money whilst letting her estate rot. She might be too weak to do anything and might not have anyone around to help her set things straight. They could be taking advantage of her. Meadwell didn't seem the type, but Tobias, he seemed clever and calculating. It was obvious he demanded a certain amount of respect and fear from Miss Meadwell.

It could be true. They might have kicked themselves into gear when they heard me and my mum were coming. I'd need to find Mrs Woods and question her, but that was easier said than done. Since my arrival I hadn't seen her at all and aside from a few bumps and knocks from the rooms above mine I wouldn't even assume she was here at all had I not been told.

I sat in the pleasant undergrowth mulling over my own paranoid thoughts when the a chilling feeling of being watched suddenly came over me. The sound of a twig snapping and the suggestion of movement from the corner of my eye snapped me back into reality and I froze. My stomach churned from the sudden rush of adrenaline and I slowly turned my head, fearful of what was squatting out of view, a sickening voyeur hidden in the woods like a horror cliché from a low budget eighties slasher flick.

As I was finally able to see my watcher, my anxious fear melted away into that of pure wonder and amazement. Probably only ten feet away from me was the exquisite form of a young fawn, its white speckles glowing in the shadows of the trees as the sun beams reflected from its delicate coat. It observed me with black, marble eyes as its ears twitched and turned towards me with curiosity. I sat as still as a Roman statue, not wanting to startle the gentle creature. I felt like a princess as this beautiful beast had approached me without fear, choosing to investigate this strange intruder.

It took a few tentative steps forward, sniffing the air between us and hoped my sweaty stench wouldn't scare it away. I raised my hand tediously slow, reaching out, hoping it would accept my sign of friendship. The fawn continued to advance and my heart rate increased. I felt a stupid grin stretch across my face. Then, without warning the fawn halted, raising its head and looking into the woods before bounding away in a few energetic hops. It stopped again further into the trees looking back towards me, almost as though it were signalling for me to follow. Or, at least that's what I assumed it was doing.

I gently stood up, ignoring the pins and needles that buzzed through my right leg like the static of an old, out of tune TV. I edged forwards, all the while under the watchful gaze of my fawn friend. As I moved past the treeline the fawn bounced away a few paces, keeping just ahead of me. I moved a little more quickly and discovered I was walking along an old, disused path, overgrown with ivy and ferns. I felt like a jungle explorer who stumbled upon an ancient path that lead to the ruins of some unknown tribe.

I tripped over a rotten branch and the fawn, startled, broke into a run, agilely navigating its way through the dense growth of trees and plants and sprinting out of view. I was no longer too concerned. I knew it would run away eventually and now my attention had turned to my discovery of the lost path. Mum always did say I had the attention span of a gnat.

The path was hard to follow, covered by the moist leaves, dirt and dust of decades of disuse. I had to walk hunched over and concentrate on where it was leading me, stepping in between the sinew like tendrils and roots. I don't remember how long I was walking, but a sudden feeling of dread came over me that I cannot explain. I came to a kind of clearing in the dense woodlands and looked up to examine the area.

Squatting before me in the thick bushes, ensnared in twisted branches and suffocating vines was a dilapidated, ugly shed made up of rotten wooden planks and rusted nails. The one window that peered through the dirt was boarded up and splashed with black, blinding it to my approach. I tentatively moved forward, unconsciously thinking this is somewhere I shouldn't be. The leaves above me rustled together as a silent breeze manoeuvred through the clearing, disturbing a light mist that loitered just above the ground.

I wondered what was inside, my childish curiosity getting the better of my adult sensibility. I moved to examine the door and found it to be made of new, untreated but strong wood. The scent of freshly cut pine filled my nose and brought with it memories of hot summer days spent milling around DIY stores and garden centres, looking to buy that years collection of expensive plants, only for them to starve to death during the winter months. I found it strange, but even more so that a heavy duty, reinforced steel padlock prevented me from forcing my way inside. A million thoughts and questions populated my mind, only to be ejected swiftly seconds later.

An eerie moan emanated from within the shed. Quiet at first forcing me to hold my breath. It could have been an animal, a fox perhaps moaning from the unbearable heat or calling to another for aid. Perhaps it was hurt. I turned my head, focusing my ear towards the cracks in the splintered, moss covered planks of the shed wall. There was movement inside and then, an ear splitting scream. I stumbled backwards and my skin almost leapt from my body wanting to flee. It could have been human, or something human like but bestial in its fear and pain. A tortured soul screamed out as though it had been sliced or skewered before a merciless taskmaster.

I fumbled on the ground, pushing myself to my feet and dashing away in an aimless direction. Fuck knows which way I came from, all I knew was which way I needed to run from. The woodlands became thicker the more I ran, spiteful branches grasped at my shirt and whipped my legs. I could have been running through a field of stinging nettles but I didn't care, I had to escape from the creature in the shed. Flashes of great, lumbering beasts bolting through the door and giving chase spurred me on. My vision became a blur of browns and greens as I ran full pelt before tumbling out into the open and crashing into someone. I screamed as their strong hands gripped my upper arms.

"Let me go!"

“Whoa whoa whoa, just calm down a minute,” came the deep, relaxing tone of the stranger I had collided with.

He looked down at me with dark, green eyes which reflected the bright sunlight making them shine like emeralds. They were framed by long, dark lashed and his shaggy brown hair swept across his brow, framing his handsome face. He wore a loose, dirty white vest from which his muscular arms erupted and fastened on to mine, holding me steady. I felt my face begin to burn with embarrassment.

“What are you running from?” He asked, his a face twisted portrait of concern and confusion.

“Nothing, no one,” I stuttered out, still shaking slightly from the adrenaline pumping through my body. “None of your business really. Who the fuck are you anyway?”

“Huh, you’re polite,” He said, not seeming irritated at my stupid reaction. “Jonah.”

“*Jonah*? What are you, like an Amish or something?”
His laugh was cute, deep but light and somehow calmed me.

“No, but my parents are very, well, religious I guess. And who the fuck are you?” He imitated.
I smiled, impressed by his banter.

“Bea, if you must know.”

“Bea?” He questioned with a mischievous smile.

“Shut up.” I had always hated my name. It was an old womans name but my mum seemed to think that old names were coming back into fashion. It could have been worse I guess.

"So you're Mrs Wood's great niece or something then?" Asked Jonah as he finally let go of my arms. I looked him up and down, I guess he was handsome, if you were into the muscular farm boy kind of guys.

"Yeah, and what about you? Are you my long lost cousin?"

Please don't be my long lost cousin.

"Haha no," he said. Thank God. "My family live on a farm down the road. I help out Mr Imamu in the gardens for a bit of extra cash every now and again."

"Mr Imamu?"

"Yeah, he's the grounds keeper. You must have seen him. Old African guy, pretty hench for his age."

I knew who he was talking about and my previous anxiety came back as to whether I came across as racist or not came back to me.

"Oh, yeah I've seen him. I don't think he likes me."

"I wonder why. Did you ask him who the fuck he was as well?"

I smiled. I don't know if it was because he was the first moderately attractive guy I'd seen in weeks, or whether I was just happy to talk to someone who seemed half normal, but there was something about Jonah that made me want to open up. I felt instantly comfortable around him, like I could tell him everything. And yeah, I was a little attracted to him. Of course, the pleasantries didn't last. Just as the memories of my horrific encounter in the woodlands began to disappear, another scream tore through the quiet summer air.

We both turned in unison to face the house, the look of terror on my face mirrored in his. It was a female scream, a scream of pain and fear. He ran off, heading towards the house and there was nothing I could do but follow him, but I did wonder why we were heading towards the danger.

CHAPTER 5

I sprinted as fast as I could after Jonah, he slowed slightly, turning to make sure I was behind him, his face his face red and dripping with panic. We reached the back door which lead into the kitchen and cautiously made our way inside. My heart was racing, partly from the brief bout of exercise my body wasn't used to and partly from the absolute dread that was nestled in my stomach The kitchen was empty, save for a steaming kettle sat on the hob and a sink full of dirty dishes left from breakfast. Mumbled, agitated voices floated through from the adjacent room.

Jonah looked through an opposite doorway, obviously not hearing what I had. I cautiously peered around the darkwood door frame into the sitting room where the perturbed sounds originated from. The room was dark, heavy curtains partially drawn over the tall windows, the bright light locked mostly out and that which penetrated the gloom highlighted old, worn arm chairs and end tables. The orange light from an antique desk lamp lit to figures huddled in the corner. One was seated in a wheelchair, quietly whimpering and quivering. The other was a tall man, dressed smartly and busying himself with a towel.

He noticed that he was being watched and turned to look at me. Caught in the act of peeping I revealed myself from around the corner.

"Miss Hammond, what are you doing here?" He asked. Tobias. Creeping around in the dark with a feeble old woman.

"Maybe I should ask you the same question," I replied defiantly, glaring at him through the dimness.

"And what exactly are you insinuating with that?" He asked annoyed.

Jonah appeared behind me, finally realising I had discovered the source of our investigation. He may be pretty, but I guess he doesn't have much awareness of things going on around him.

"We heard the scream, what are you doing with her?"

Tobias flung open a heavy set of curtains and bright light radiated the room, causing me to squint, as did the wrinkled old woman shuddering in the wheelchair. I heard steps behind me and Miss Meadwell trotted into view from another corridor.

"What am I doing?" Tobias mocked, his face clearly vexed as his face turned an angry shade of red. "Dear Mrs Woods here managed to spill her freshly brewed cup of Earl Grey onto her lap. I was merely assisting her by cleaning up the mess before the hot tea scalded her."

Mrs Woods, or, Great Aunt Woods I should say, turned towards me, her eyes cloudy and sunken, her cheek bones prominent as the wrinkled skin hung loosely from the bones with the rest of her body hidden under a thick, chequered blanket.

"I'm fine," she gasped looking through me. "I'm fine, I'm fine."

"Isn't she hot in that blanket?" I asked, it must have been almost thirty degrees outside.

"As I already stated, Mrs Woods is feeling under the weather," Tobias said almost mockingly. "She has become very weak due to it and we must take extra precautions against the infections. I'm sure you're aware members of the geriatric community feel the cold a lot more than those of the younger generation. Miss Meadwell, would you please take Mrs Woods to the bathroom and get her cleaned up."

"Yes sir," came the timid response like it had been voiced by a shrew.

As Meadwell exited the room, pushing the creaking old chair, Tobias' eyes followed until they became fixed on a certain point. His eyes widened and his brow furrowed when he noticed the small amount of mud on the floor. He turned his furious gaze upon Jonah.

"Boy! How many times must I tell you to stay out of the house, lest you trail the entire gardens through my polished floors!" He erupted. Jonah looked down at his feet and back up to Tobias, shrugging in a half arse kind of apology. "Get out!" He yelled.

Jonah casually jogged away, turning to wink at me with those lovely, stupid, dark eyes.

"There's not that much mud," I said. "And your floors aren't that well polished."

"Would you care to do it better yourself?"

"I'd rather not."

"Then watch your tongue Miss Hammond." Although I prodded and poked him, he seemed to be calming himself down. The throbbing vein on the side of his head subsiding as he breathed through his nose. "Now, you'd do well to be careful around that boy." He cautioned. "He may not seem bright, but he is very cunning when it comes to getting what he wants."

"And what is it that he wants?" I asked in the best impression of the Queen's English I could muster.

"I'm sure I need not tell you," he said looking at me plainly. "And I'm sure I need not remind you of how you mother would react if she were to return to her daughter being impregnated by the local farm boy."

I blushed, of course I knew what he was talking about but I hadn't expected a prude like Tobias to come right out and say it.

"Now, go and occupy yourself elsewhere while I clean up this mess."

I quickly walked away rubbing my arms. The whole conversation had made me feel awkward and I needed to get away from his stupid, sly face. I had only known Jonah for a few moments and as annoying as Tobias was he had known him longer. Maybe all Jonah did want was to get in my knickers. But maybe he was a nice guy and Tobias was just finding another way to ruin my life. Did I really care?

I wandered through the hallways and up the stairs mulling things over. Even if Jonah did only want one thing, there wasn't much else to do around here. I mean, I'm not that kind of girl and I definitely wouldn't give it up easily. Or at all. But this place was sucking the life out of me with nothing to do. If I wasn't careful I'd end up like Aunt Woods.

The more I thought about her the more unsettled I felt. She looked like a corpse sat in that chair, I doubt she even knew what day of the week it was. How long had she been like that? I wondered if Mum knew how bad she was. I didn't even know the woman but I couldn't help but feel concern for her well-being.

As I rounded a corner and walked down a dimly lit corridor I came to a stop at the end of a narrow set of bare, wooden stairs. My concerns for the doddering old woman were drained from me completely and replaced by another, unwelcome feeling. As I looked up into the unlit stairwell, one feature was evident, staring down at me tauntingly. My hairs stood on end and I couldn’t remove my eyes from what loomed above me. A bright, red door. The red door from my dream the night before.

My knees trembled as the memory of the dream returned to me in horrific detail. I spun around quickly, half expecting the mummified corpse to be waiting for me, preparing to drag its foetid form towards me, but thankfully there was nothing. I ran, ran as fast as I could. I couldn’t explain it but i knew there was something wrong with that door, or whatever was behind it. I returned to my room and slammed the door behind me, confining myself there for the rest of the day. There was no way I could have seen the door before, I had not been to that floor of the house so how was it possible that I had dreamed of it in such detail? As the sun set I dared not sleep, fearful of every tiny noise that escaped from the old house, every squeak that could alert me to that dreaded door opening and the nightmare held behind it being loosed.

CHAPTER 6

As the sun rose the next day it brought with it grey clouds and rain. To say it was torrential would be an understatement. It was like the whole fucking ocean was pouring from the sky, which was a bit of a relief as the heat was becoming unbearable. But even with the rain it still felt hot. I felt like a zombie when Miss Meadwell gently knocked on my door in the morning to wake me. I was already awake, I think, I'm not sure if I slept or not during the night. I faintly recall strange dreams, blurs of colour and movement but nothing really cohesive, not like my previous dreams since I got here.

As I drank down the remaining sloppy mixture of milk, Weetabix and sugar from breakfast I was actually happy to see Tobias as he informed me I had a phone call waiting from my mum. I practically raced through the house into the main entrance hall where an antique rotary phone sat with its receiver resting against the dusty, glass console. I snatched it and pressed the blue plastic to my ear.

"Mum?"

"Oh, my Bumble Bea, it's so nice to hear your voice again."

"Calm down mum, it's only been like, two days," I said like a typical teenage brat. Really I missed her too, more than I thought I would have done. I felt isolated here in the huge mansion, hundreds of miles from any true remnants of civilisation with no one but the odd ensemble of house staffing watching over me.

"I know I know, it's just, since we left together we've gotten closer than… well, never mind. How are things there?" There was real sadness in her voice which broke my heart.

"It's boring here so you'd better hurry up and get back," I complained, hiding my own sadness and sitting on the bottom step of the main staircase. "I literally can't do anything without having being told or having to ask first. It's like a prison."

"Oh honey, it can't be that bad," she reassured.

"Oh Mum, it is. And this house is so weird. They're forever cleaning it but it seems like it hasn't been properly cleaned in weeks. I don't trust Tobias either."

"Tobias means well, he just has a lot of things to take care of."

"I don't know. And Great Aunt Woods, there's something wrong with her, did they tell you how ill she really is, or what's wrong with her exactly?"

"Yes they did. Listen Bea, Aunt Woods is a very old lady, but I'm sure she will be better soon. Until then, please try not to cause any trouble."

Why does everybody assume I'm going to cause trouble? I'm seventeen for Christ's sake, not a child. I was always a good girl growing up. I never did any drugs, never smoked, never got into any trouble really. I didn't want to argue with her, I was so happy to hear her voice I didn't want to ruin the conversation.

"So how are things going with finding Dad?" I asked, changing the subject but getting a horrible feeling in my stomach when I remembered the reason why I was even here at all.

"It's going well, the police have been really helpful and finally believe me. They found CCTV footage of him at a petrol station a little further up north and are investigating that. Hopefully they'll find him soon and we can get this mess sorted out for good."

"I hope so, I miss you mum." I suppose there's no harm in actually letting her know. She breathed heavily down the phone.

"I miss you too honey. Listen, I've got to go. Try not to worry, and try to have fun. It's a big house, I'm sure you'll find something to do. I love you and I'll call you again when I can."

"Love you too mum, bye."

The disappointing drone of the phone line sounded as she hung up. I lazily and reluctantly replaced the receiver and looked around. She was right, this place was big. I thought about exploring it a little but was perturbed by the thought of that menacing red door. But now I think about it, am I certain I dreamt about the door at all? I remember reading somewhere that we don't always perceive colour in our dreams, that our brain fills it in after we wake up. It could have been any colour and I just assumed it was red when I saw a similar door in the house. But it did seem so real, and looked exactly the same.

I had to do something. Outside was a no go unless I had an ark or something to float around in. Fuck it. I gathered myself and ventured up the huge, dark wood staircase onto the first floor, determined to find something to do, even if I didn't go up another floor. I searched the corridors trying all of the doors. Some were locked and the handles clean, I assumed they were the staff's rooms. Other door handles were covered in a thick layer of dust, creaking in protest as I turned them. Most were bedrooms, bed's made, boring old people decor, nothing unusual. Other's were empty store rooms, filled with brooms, mops, buckets, piles of cardboard boxes containing countless lost memories. The usual.

Eventually I stumbled upon a room worth investigating. Through a set of mahogany double doors, beautifully carved with floral patterns, I found a library. And not just a few books, but many shelves of leather bound tomes and volumes. It was like something you'd expect to see in a castle. I wasn't normally much of a big reader nowadays, preferring a trashy magazine than a classic novel, but there was a time when I'd sit up in my room reading Enid Blyton or Roald Dahl hours before bedtime. Maybe now was the best time to get back into it.

I began to walk up and down the aisles, examining the names of the books as I walked. I had to wipe some clear from dust and muck in order to see but they were all so old. Antique encyclopedias of gardening, preparations of turnips for roasting, the good carpet compendium. Really gripping stuff. There were quite a few fiction books, but I didn't recognise any of the others and they were titled with Italian names or foreign cities and just didn't interest me. I flicked through a few and became disheartened at the lack of pictures, which I knew was childish but how else do they expect to attract readers.

I continued walking, subconsciously skimming over titles printed onto the spines of the books when my eyes suddenly focused. It had picked up a word that brought my vacant mind into focus. Witchcraft. Now we're talking. A book on the history of witchcraft is something I could sink my teeth into. I looked further along the shelf and found a few more oddly occult texts, bound in black and red leathers with Latin titles, faded so they became obscure. Some very old and in such a state of disrepair their pages were practically falling out. Why the hell would my Great Aunt need books about witches and demons?

The floorboard creaked and my head quickly snapped to the left as I vaguely caught the glimpse of someone, or something dart behind the shelves. I jogged to the end of the aisle and saw nothing. The room was still empty, the door closed. I was tired, maybe my mind was playing tricks on me, although this weird house did seem to have some unusual affect on my mind.

Just as I relaxed the sound of books tumbling to the ground startled me, causing me to return to my previous position beside the weird collection of taboo texts. One book had fallen to the floor, I'd probably disturbed it whilst fumbling through the others. Picking it up and turning it around I found it to be titled '*Legiones Inferni'*. At least that's what I think it was called, the words were so badly worn in the crisp, cow hide cover they were difficult to make out.

The bent spine groaned as I spread the pages gently, they were yellow and thin like the dried out leaves of autumn, some crumbling at the edges. I couldn't understand the text, written in some strange combination of Latin and hieroglyphs but thankfully there were images to help me decipher what knowledge the book kept. There were drawings of strange creatures, humanoid but with various differences to the usual homosapian physiology. Some had great, bat like wings, others had sharp, cruel beaks and rending claws. Horrific amalgamations of man and monster, demons. It was some kind of hellish encyclopedia or grimoire.

The images fascinated me, I felt like I was some kind of sneaky voyeur, nervous at being caught looking at something I shouldn't, like a young boy who had stumbled upon his dad's secret porno stash. Curiously I noticed that part way through the book a large number of pages had been torn out. I looked around the floor, underneath the bookcase and along the shelves attempting to locate the missing sheets but with no success. I decided I would sneak the book back to my room for a closer look, for some reason I had the feeling Tobias wouldn't be too happy if he knew I was taking things from their proper place, but this odd collection of blasphemous texts didn't make sense to me. In a library full of boring books about housekeeping, gardening and the likes, why would my ninety year old great aunt have a number of satanic scriptures?

That night I hurriedly finished my meal, eager to return to my room and pour through my secret treasure. I often ate alone anyway, but usually took my time in consuming whatever awful creation Miss Meadwell had concocted. The woman could just about muster up an adequate breakfast but when it came to other, more taxing forms of culinary delights, her expertise seemed a little lacking. I never saw the staff eating but assumed they ate later after I had finished, which seemed a little old fashioned to me but I didn't mind. The last thing I wanted was to engage in petty small talk with people I didn't even like.

With my stomach full I rushed upstairs, throwing off my clothes and climbing into something more comfortable. My pits were less than fresh but I had decided a shower could wait until the next day, the water would probably be cold by now anyway and there were always huge spiders in the corners of the bathroom ceiling, unapologetically observing me. I opened my window, it had stopped raining by dinner time and as the sun set a chorus of frogs had began their squeaking symphony out in the fields, brought out by the moisture of the recent downpour. I closed the curtains, clicked on the bedside lamp and retrieved my secret tome from underneath the bed.

Loosely wrapped in the bed sheet's I began flicking through the pages once again, racking my brain in an attempt to remember the basic Latin we were forced to learn when I was a child. It was futile, the few words I could remember were so ambiguous that they would probably never be used in an actual sentence. The more I read, they heavier my eyes became. I struggled on, widening my lids in an attempt to stave of sleep. In all honesty I dreaded falling asleep, since I'd been here the strange nightmares had started to affect my mental state and I wasn't prepared to face them again.

But I should have known it was useless. The inevitable embrace of slumber swept over me like a heavy blanket and within moments my head had rocked back and my eyes had closed firmly, plummeting me into a world of blackness, inviting in the unnerving visions I had expected and feared.

CHAPTER 7

I opened my eyes. I was lay on my bed, as I was before but something was different. I couldn't figure it out at first as my gaze drifted over the antique decor of the bedroom, my meagre belongings scattered over the floor and furniture. And then realisation swept over me. I was dreaming. The room around me dissolved into nothingness, a dense black curtain that surrounded and threatened to suffocate me. I was adrift on the colourless ocean, sat on my bed, desperately clutching the old, moth eaten sheet as my head spun and I began to panic.

There was nothing but the utter silence, aside from my own whimpering breaths echoing in the void, until the subtle sounds of footsteps rung through the nothingness. Steady and implacable, they approached me as I threw my head from side to side, trying to determine which direction this unknown assailant was approaching from. I stupidly called out for them to show themselves and instantly questioned why I would do that. I suppose having something in front of you is less terrifying that it being unknown. A figure began to appear in the gloom, almost like a faint light with a malformed blob at its centre. As the footsteps increased in volume, so too did the shape that was the centre of the light take a more definite form.

It was a person, undeniably male from the shape of his broad shoulders and square shape. I squinted as the light became almost blinding. The stranger finally approached the foot of my bed, seemingly walking on thin air in the darkness and the sharp light dimmed, allowing me to cast my eyes on the individual before me. He smiled down at me gently, his dark eyes comforting me and I felt the fear melt away from inside of me. Suddenly the darkness wasn't something to be afraid of, it was warm and safe, isolating and cradling the two of us. Jonah and I.

He crawled onto the bed and up until now I hadn't realised that he was completely naked. His body was lean, his muscular arms tensing as he crawled towards me, the darkness obscuring his nether regions. I leaned back against the pillow as he moved over me, still smiling. I could smell his scent, sweet and manly. Normally the smell of sweat would make me want to vomit, but coming from Jonah it kind of turned me on. I hadn't realised how attractive he was, but I knew secretly that I wanted this to happen.

His face moved quickly and I found his lips pressed against my own, his wet tongue pushing between my lips and wrapping itself around mine. I didn't know how I should react at first but then it came naturally. I kissed back, I enjoyed it. I held onto his rippling, broad back as he slowly but purposefully unbuttoned the oversized white shirt I had been wearing for bed, exposing my breast and grabbing them vigorously with his rugged hands.

But then he stopped. He froze in place, the look on his face, where his hands were. A complete halt. I kissed his neck but elicited no response. My hands dropped.

"J-Jonah?" I asked timidly, brushing back a wild lock of hair that had fallen over my face in the heated passion.

He said nothing, did nothing except continue to stare and smile at me. But then his smile faded, his mouth became straight and the warm, comforting look in his eye faded away to complete nothingness. The skin on his neck moved and I saw, from behind his left ear, something begin to materialise.

It was a repulsive pinkish grey colour, a long, boney set of fingers. The skin hung from them in flaps like a cheap packet of wafer thin ham. The nails were yellow and split as they dug viciously into Jonah's neck. He showed no signs of pain as the hand extended fully around his throat, accompanied by a horrific, gurgling, wheezing sound from behind. The stench of burnt flesh made me recoil, the acidic taste of vomit filling my mouth as I pushed away, into the pillows piled high behind me.

Jonah slowly stood up, either by his own accord or lead by the decayed hand clutched firmly around his neck. He stumbled backwards and I heard the wet, slapping sound of another persons steps behind him, hidden by Jonah's manly form, now dreadfully pale and shivering as he moved away from the bed. Tears streamed down my face as I sat alone, afraid and seemingly unable to prevent the events unfolding before me.

"Leave him alone!" I shouted desperately, holding together my shirt as I knelt up. It was an animalistic scream of tears and saliva.

Jonah stopped moving, his eyes rolled back in there sockets, leaving only the whites exposed as his head lolled back lazily and his limbs became limp. The creature behind him quivered and pulled Jonah aside slightly, revealing its gruesome form. It too was naked, but completely repulsive, the same decayed, rotten thing that had cornered me at the foot of the stairs which lead up towards the red door. A half decomposed female figure, the skin hanging like dried leather, her breasts like sacks of dust, the skin a mixture of pale yellows and sore pinks. The flesh around her face had melted away, leaving only a wet lump of gore and saliva as she gurgled at me with malice, squeezing the throat of beautiful Jonah threateningly.

"Please, please don't hurt him," I begged, and strangely, I thought for a moment I saw a tear fall from the creatures pale, milky eyes before moments later they both burst into flames. Searing, scorching plumes of orange rolled up into the darkness, redefining the confines of the room, scarring the ceiling with soot and setting the walls alight. The bodies disappeared in the bright light of the flames. I screamed, screamed as my throat dried out from the heat. My lungs exploded and my skin bubbled as the fire engulfed the bed, stripping the flesh from my bones and as my eyeballs began to melt my eyelids shot open.

*

I was lay in bed, the room lit not by flames but from the cold light of the moon. The sheets were wet from sweat yet I was freezing cold. My eyes stung from tears and my heart was almost leaping from my chest pounding so fiercely I feared it would never calm again. I dared not close my eyes again that night, I lay clutching myself in the sickly light of the bedside lamp, full of terror, buttoning up the white shirt I had worn for bed.

CHAPTER 8

A crystal bead of sweat rolled down my forehead, landing on the ancient towel that smelled faintly of piss from being stored in a dank cupboard for God knows how long. I lay out in the sun, warming my body, trying to recharge after another sleepless night. I was beginning to get dark rings under my eyes and my complexion was horrid. It felt safer to close my eyes during the day, outside in the sun, away from that giant monstrosity of a house.

All signs of rain clouds had completely disappeared and the sky was and endless sapphire ocean, the only landscape the impossibly bright orb of sunlight perched in the centre, its hot rays hammering down on the Earth below. The ground was already bone dry and it was only eleven o'clock. I wiped the sweat from my forehead and sat up to take a drink of warm water from the bottle beside me.

I looked down the garden and could see a figure busying himself in a small tool shed. It was Mr Imamu, the gardener. I had bumped into him this morning and made an effort to engage in conversation, attempting to rectify my previous mistake of avoiding him. He seemed pleasant enough but wasn't much for chit chat. He responded to my small talk politely but in a very thick African accent that I struggled to identify. It could have been Somalian, Nigerian, I couldn't quite place it. I grew up in a small, northern mining town, primarily populated by working class white men and women. I hadn't had much experience identifying accents and dialects outside of Britain.

I decided that out of the three house staff I had met, Mr Imamu had been my favourite. Miss Meadwell was just too quiet and nervous for my liking, I couldn't quite figure her out, unlike Mr Imamu. He was to the point but polite and had even brought me the bottle of water after he noticed I had been lying in the sunlight, warning me of heat stroke or something. I Wasn't too bothered but it was a nice gesture I suppose.

I watched him as he fumbled with something before placing it on the ground and standing back. Moments later a small, orange creature emerged from the nearby bushes. It moved over to the container Imamu had placed on the ground. It was a fox cub, and it was eating a small amount of food, placed there by the gardener who crouched down with a huge, kind grin on his face.

He reached out gently and the fox cub approached without caution, sniffing Imamus' huge paw before nuzzling into the fist. I had never seen a wild animal act so friendly with a person before, it was unbelievable.

"It's rude to spy on people you know," Came a voice from behind me.

I quickly spun around, squinting behind my sunglasses to see Jonah stood above me, hands on hips. His shirt was undone down to his belly button, revealing his muscular upper body. He was deliciously toned, athletic and the sweat on his skin caused it to glisten in the sunlight, it made my insides quiver.

"Well why the fuck are you spying on me then?" I snapped.

"How could I not when you're dressed in those tight little shorts," he said with a playful wink.

"So I guess Tobias was right about you then."

"I'm just joking, that toff doesn't know a thing about me." His face changed, becoming more serious, I guess I hit a nerve. He sat down on the grass next to me, spreading out his legs.

"Well I guess I don't know anything about you either," I said, trying to break the uncomfortable silence I had unintentionally caused.

"Well, what do you want to know?" He asked and I did that thing where you have a million questions, but as soon as you're put on the spot your mind goes blank. I ended up asking random shit instead, probably making myself look like an idiot.

"Erm, so, where do you come from?"

"I come from here," he said sarcastically. I cocked my head with a forced fake smile, informing him that he had given a stupid answer to a stupid question. I didn't have to say anything and he elaborated. "I live on a farm just down the road, as you know, with very religious parents, as you know. There's not much else to it, I was homeschooled and spent most of my life around here. I prefer the country to busy towns anyway, it's just so much quieter and relaxed out here." He lay back with his arms behind his head, his biceps bulging. I couldn't help but think of the dream I had, his naked body, it was strangely accurate considering I hadn't really spent that much time looking at Jonah before.

"Don't you ever get bored out here? There's nothing to do."

"There's plenty to do, it's just different to what you'd do in the city."

"Hmm, I'm not convinced," I complained, pulling my knees up to my chest. "So, why doesn't Tobias like you then?"

"Probably because he knows I don't like him either," he said frankly, sitting up again. "He took the place of the previous head of house, an old guy that was pretty cool, a lot friendlier, but wasn't very strict. It's probably why the house is in the state it's in now. Tobias has been here just under a year now and he's constantly keeping Meadwell and Mr Imamu busy. I help where I can, but I can't always be away from home too long, farming is hard work you know."

"I don't trust Tobias," I confessed, unsure whether I should voice my opinions or not, but not really giving a fuck. "I get the feeling he's up to something, I don't know if it has anything to do with my great aunt being ill or not.

"Well, she's never really been ill before, but she is pretty fucking old."

"Yeah, I know. It doesn't matter." I felt stupid for saying that.

"So what about you, why are you here?" Jonah asked and I suddenly felt nervous. I probably shouldn't tell him my dad went full on psycho, tried to beat my mum to a pulp and kidnap me.

"Oh, just family stuff. I won't be here long."

"That's a shame, the view has improved an awful lot since you arrived."

I threw him a smile, blatant flirting and objectification of me would usually result in me tearing a guys head off and throwing all manner of profanities towards him, but for some reason it only made me like Jonah more.

"You need to calm yourself," I said standing up and stretching, knowing he was watching me. "I'm going inside to get a drink, I think your break is over now, get back to work."

I strutted off, not looking behind because I knew Jonah would be lay there watching me. The pervert. Maybe it was just innocent flirting, if he's spent all his life out here I imagine he wouldn't have had much experience talking to girls, but he was pretty smooth. Come to think of it he was probably still a virgin like me, although *I* was through choice.

The grass felt soft between my toes, quenched by the previous days rainfall after it had almost been dried to death from the overbearing sunshine. The house loomed before me, reminding me of a prison or a gigantic beast I'd seen in some adventure film as a child, casting a dense shadow before it as the sun crowned it like a halo.

I entered the kitchen, my feet slapping against the dirty white and black chequered floor tiles. The tap squeaked and complained until a frothy jet of water gushed out and filled my empty bottle. The water tasted different here than it did in the towns and cities we drove through, less chemically. I think I prefered it. As I gulped down the water I heard the faint creak of wheels down the narrow hallway. My curiosity got the better of me and a leaned forwards to see.

The light from a large window at the end was bright, but what I saw confused me. Miss Meadwell passed quickly from one room to another, pushing Aunt Woods in her wheelchair, only this time my aunt wasn't covered in her usual thick blanket, and I saw her, her abdomen swollen and round. Almost as though she were pregnant. But that was impossible, I tried to rationalise what I saw. Perhaps it was a trick of the light, I was squinting. But what made it more real, what convinced me that what I saw was real was her hands cradling her rotund belly, stroking it gently.

CHAPTER 9

A loud, clamorous thudding caused my bedroom door to violently rumble on its hinges, stirring me from deep, dream filled sleep. The sudden noise caused me to panic as my brain strived to make sense of the sudden bombardment of sensory information. I sat up, rubbing the delightful green crust from my eyes. Miss Meadwell seemed to have gotten some strength in her weedy little arms, it seemed excessive to me to make such a noise just to get me out of bed. I know they say breakfast is the most important meal of the day but this was ridiculous.

"Miss Hammond, will you wake up!" Came the furious growl of Tobias pounding on the distressed wooden door.

"What, what is it?!" I shouted in response, my throat dry and soar as though I had been up all night screaming at the top of my lungs.

"Get dressed immediately, there is an issue with which I need to discuss with you," he ordered like an army drill sergeant. I wondered who had shoved a rod up his arse this morning. I rummaged through the neat pile of clothes that had been arranged on a chair in the corner of the room, choosing a black tank top and denim shorts. I scraped my hair into a ponytail and rubbed my eyes one last time. I probably looked like shit, but it didn't matter. I opened the door and Tobias looked down at me sternly.

"Come with me," was all he said as he turned and marched down the corridor quickly. I unenthusiastically followed after him.

"What's this about?" I asked to which I was only met with silence. I asked a number of times but gave up when it was obvious he wasn't going to answer me until we reached our destination. Ignorant. I started to recognise the part of the house we were in, I'd seen the same light and dark green striped wallpaper before, how it was bubbled and peeling at the edge. Just as I had expected we came to the large set of mahogany doors that lead into the library.

I suddenly panicked, he must know about the book that still sat hidden underneath my bed. The *Legiones Inferni*, the hellish encyclopedia of demons and hellspawn. Was it that bad I had taken a book from the library? Wasn't that what you were supposed to do? Maybe it belonged to him. He pushed open the doors and invited me to step inside with an arm extended, his cruel eyes burning into me as I walked passed.

As I entered the room I was not greeted by the rows upon rows of neatly organised books, covered in a layer of dust undisturbed, packed into antique cases, sitting proudly. Instead I was greeted with chaos. Books were strewn across the floor, pages bent, spines crooked, every inch of the floor was covered in literature. I looked around the room shocked, it was as though a huge earthquake had struck, sending the entire library plummeting to the ground. Either that or someone had been frantically searching for something, discarding the unnecessary volumes, pouring through each shelf, unsuccessful in their hunt.

Tobias made his way into the room, taking care not to trample any pages as he walked.

"Well…" He said, looking down at me disappointedly.

"Well what?" I asked, confused about the whole situation.

He sighed deeply.

"Miss Meadwell said she saw you wandering around up here two days ago."

"Right…"

"Miss Hammond, I don't know what kind of game you're playing here, but this kind of disrespectful vandalism is notappreciated and will not be left unpunished."

"Wait, you think I did this?"

"Well, how else would you explain it? Nothing of the sort occurred before your arrival here."

"But, how…"

"Enough," he interrupted. "I won't hear it. I have enough work to do without cleaning up, whatever this is supposed to be. I want you to return the books to the shelves, there should be a catalogue book somewhere in this mess. Find it and organise the shelves alphabetically as stated, to the best of you *ability.*"

Before I could even answer he turned and left, stomping down the hallway like an angry parent. This was completely unfair, I hadn't created this mess. I was particularly careful not to leave any evidence I was in the library at all. I thought back to the day and remembered I heard a strange noise, footsteps, it must have been Meadwell. I couldn't believe she ratted me out, blamed this on me. But then who had done it? I had found the *Legiones inferni* on the floor, could it be possible I had knocked them off without remembering? Surely not. I wasn't insane.

I contemplated just leaving the mess how it was, fuck Tobias, he wasn't the boss of me. I made for the door and stopped, mum would want me to behave, to do as I was told. But If I picked the books up it would be like an admission of guilt. I thought about her, sleeping alone in some shitty hotel away from her daughter, fearful of a violent husband on the loose. I didn't want to worry her anymore than she was, no doubt Tobias would inform her of my insubordination if I left the mess. I resolved to clean it up, unhappily, but would explain to Tobias later I had nothing to do with it once he had calmed down.

I began sifting through a pile close to a shelf where he had gestured the reference catalogue would be and found it rather easily. A big, black notebook, the pages old and yellowed and written in faded black ink. It detailed which books were on which shelves in what order. It would just be a case of finding the right ones, but I had no intention of being so pedantic in the order i arranged them, Tobias would just be lucky I was doing this at all.

"Wow, impressive," Came a voice from the window behind me. I screamed in surprise, turning to see Jonah's grinning face squeezed between the small gap of the partially opened window.

"Jesus Christ!" I shouted. "What the fuck are you doing?! You almost killed me!"

"Calm down calm down, I was sorting out the flower bed down there when I heard the shouting from up here. Thought I'd climb up and investigate. Are you going to let me in?"

"Well, it depends, are you going to help me clean this up?"

"Well that depends," He said with something behind his eyes that let me know he had nefarious ideas brewing in that shaggy maned head of his.

"On what?"

"On what I'll get out of it." He winked, I laughed.

"Shut the fuck up and just help me." I undid the latch and he crawled inside. "Tobias will kill you anyway if he knew you were in here dirtying up his floor so you'd better get started."

He didn't argue and we worked together through most of the day, engaging in idle chit chat. We even worked through lunch time and I hardly noticed. It was nice being able to talk with someone who was a similar age to me for once. It was great travelling with my mum, but there were some things she just wouldn't understand or that I wouldn't feel comfortable talking to her about. As perverted as Jonah would like me to believe he was, it actually turned out he was quite the gentleman, innocent and sweet. He respected his parents and worked hard. His taste in music was practically non existent but he loved to read which I found rather endearing.

He wasn't what I would call my usual type, but it seemed like it wouldn't matter if he enjoyed wrestling pigs in a paddling pool full of noodles, I'd still find myself inexplicably attracted to him. I thought about kissing him, but talked myself out of it. After all, we'd only known each other a few days, I didn't want to seem desperate, or too available. I'd leave the first move up to him, whatever happens happens I guess. The conversation flowed and was a welcome break from the overbearing weight of the nightmares I'd been having and the strange feeling I had whenever I was inside the house.

I confided in him the betrayal of Miss Meadwell and how I originally sort of liked her, I mean, we weren't best mates but she seemed nice. But now since she grassed on me I'd become bitter about her, not able to trust her. I saw her as scheming and back stabbing. Jonah tried to defend her, he told me she's just afraid of Tobias, that if she doesn't work hard enough he'll kick her out and she has nowhere else to go. She doesn't have family or really any friends to rely on. I suppose I did feel a little sympathy for her, but I couldn't help thinking, what a bitch.

The day drew on and the sun began to set, painting the sky in deep shades of purple and burnt oranges, lighting the tops of the trees on fire as the moon began to peer from distant clouds. We had practically finished replacing the books and eagerly stuffed the final copies back into their timber abodes.

"Finally," I gasped. "Do you think Aunt Woods has actually read all of these?"

"I doubt it," Jonah scoffed. "Some of them sound so boring they'd be better off in the fireplace."

"Wait, there's something wrong," I said, silencing Jonah's light hearted jokes. I'd spent all day looking at the covers, spines and names of thousands of books and something struck me. I walked up and down the shelves, my eyes skimming over the book titles. Nothing. The odd collection of occult books was missing entirely. No trace of them remained. I explained to Jonah about the books and he simply laughed, asking why an old woman would need books on demons and magic rituals. He said I was losing my mind.

I know he was joking, but what if I really was. I'd had hardly any sleep since coming here, plagued by nightmares and horrific visions. What I thought was real could be pure fantasy. They say when you're insane you don't realise it, but does me now thinking it mean I'm not? The sun set and Jonah left through the window he entered, not wanting to get caught by Tobias who had not intruded the entire day, not even to collect me for lunch. I made my way downstairs and ate a bland dinner of boiled vegetables, dried chicken and lumpy mash. Miss Meadwell wouldn't make eye contact with me, she couldn't. Tobias glared at me before leaving, obviously still angry and not wanting to talk. Whatever.

I returned to my room and threw myself on the bed. Was I going crazy? I wished my mum was here, all I wanted to do was to hug her and leave this place. The house, the people, they were getting inside my head, scrambling my brain and insulting me for it. I hung my head from the side and looked underneath. The *Legiones Inferni* lay there in the darkness, physical and tangible. It was proof that the books where there, so where were they now? Had Meadwell hidden them?

CHAPTER 10

Darkness, tangible darkness that melted away like oil draining from the road to reveal a twisted mockery of the bedroom gave me all the indication I needed to realise I was dreaming again. The room was drenched in a blueish green hue and the furniture seemed to vibrate, their edges almost incorporeal. The smell of burning smoke faintly filled the room and I began to panic that the house was on fire. I couldn't see smoke, or feel any heat. I listened carefully for the sound of crackling flame, but instead I could have sworn I could hear the distant cries of a baby.

I rose from the bed deciding to investigate the situation, nervous as I was I seemed to have some control over my actions in the dream, I was aware. The bedroom door clicked and creaked, the handle turned and it slowly opened. I stared intensely, thinking

I should look for something to defend myself with but was only frozen in place. There was nobody there, the hallway outside dark and empty save for one sound. A voice, or the memory of a voice. Quiet, like the sound of the breeze, whispering for me to follow it.

There was no malice behind the voice, no signs of evil intent, but there was urgency. It wanted me to pursue it, it needed me to. Against my better judgement I walked out the room towards the beckoning voice. The house was not how I remembered it in the waking world. No light shone through the darkened windows, there was only a void behind the glass, a swirling mass of nothingness that I dared not look into for fear of the abyss looking back. The wallpaper had peeled and the plaster beneath was cracked and chipped, a dark brown, viscous liquid seeping from the wounds.

Picture frames hung at jaunty angles, the images within them faded or warped into things not human, twisted figures in pink and red lights, writhing in pain and agony. The further I walked the blues and greens darked, transformed into deep purples, oranges and crimson reds. The brown liquid flowed more fervently, oozing from every possible crack and seam, pooling along the edges of the corridor, its hue turning into a deep, reddy black, the metallic smell making me feel nauseous. The infant's cries increased in volume, screaming as if tormented, and still the voice beckoned.

I ascended misshapen staircases, their angular steps seeming unstable but solid, and as I elevated I felt as though I were descending. I couldn't explain it or describe the feeling. My heart raced as the house transformed into something from a horror film but I was pulled forward by the pleading voice. It begged me to keep going, it told me I needed to see, to witness. I needed to understand.

"Understand what?" I asked, but it did not reply, just continued to beg, continued to persuade.

I rounded a corner, my feet sticky with the red liquid from the bleeding walls, lumps of congealed fluid stuck between my toes and I looked up. Before me was the narrow staircase, the red door illuminated at the top. Only this time, the door opened. Slowly, menacingly. I didn't want to be here, I needed to run. Whatever was behind there, every fibre of my body, every cell screamed that it was evil, that I shouldn't enter the room. But the voice told me to climb the stairs, to enter the room. It was the only way to end the nightmare.

Surely I would wake up eventually, I didn't have to subject myself to terror in order to wake. As I deliberated the hallways began to fill, the liquid was ankle deep and the screams of the child grew more furious, they emanated from the blackness behind the red door and the smell of burning wood intensified. The voice had become quiet, I called out to it but only the infants cries replied.

"Wake up, wake up, wake up, wake up," I repeated, pinching my legs and arms, bruising my skin but nothing worked. I wasn't waking that easily.

The lights at the end of the hallways began to dim and against my instincts I took a step forward, closer to the yawning opening atop the stairs. My stomach again churned, I felt that if I were to lift up my top I would see the skin undulating and squirming. My heart raced and I felt light headed. Eventually I reached the top and steadied myself against the door frame. A cautionary glance behind me revealed that the corridor which lead me here had now been filled with a thick, black liquid, bubbling and swirling, sealing off my escape. There was only one direction to go now.

I stepped into the darkness of the room, all sounds disappeared. It was as though I had placed a cup over my ears, the air seemed to echo, muffled and strange. I walked forward, seeing nothing of my surroundings save for a strip of light from the doorway that stretched before me, absorbed by the rough wooden floor. Reflecting the light were a few dots of crimson liquid, like small, red marbles. I followed the dotted trail to a small pool, then a river. The blood was flowing from somewhere or someone. I tentatively moved forwards, following the bloody trail.

I heard her before I saw her, her ragged breaths floating through the air, wheezing, struggling to fill her lungs. She lay naked, her flesh burned and blistered, red sores and purple bruises covering her. Her colour was indistinguishable, soaked and matted with coagulated blood, stuck to her head. She lay on a soiled, bloody mattress, her legs spread and the river of blood oozing from the shadow there. Her abdomen was swollen, huge, larger than I could ever imagine a woman's belly could stretch. From underneath the skin something writhed, it tossed and turned, it was alive within her. Her head rocked, her eyes flickered open exposing the whites before her pupils focused on me and she lurched up, supporting her weight on her massicated arms.

"Please," she rasped through cracked, dry lips. "Kill. Kill it, kill me. P-please."

I held my hands to my face, partly through shock and partly to keep myself from vomiting.

"Please!" She screamed. "He's here!"

I stepped forward but froze in place when I realised we weren't alone. She wept as I looked into the darkness behind her. Seven feet from the floor were two, glowing, ruby eyes. I looked into those eyes and felt all control leave my body. My blood boiled, attempting to force its way out of my veins, trying to escape and my insides convulsed violently. I was filled with perfect dread by the complete evilness expressed in those eyes. The darkness came alive, altered into a choking smoke that swirled around the room, stretching out like tendrils that moved to surround me.

I stepped backwards, my limbs trembling and the eyes flashed with pure rage and a thunderous, inhuman voice bellowed from all directions.

"GET OUT!"

*

I lurched up in bed, soaking wet from sweat, my limbs shaking and my heart racing. I felt a wetness between my legs and quickly fumbled to remove the covers. The white sheets had been stained yellow, as well as the shorts I slept in. Emotion flooded me and tears streamed from my eyes. What the fuck was happening to me?

As the thought entered my mind an excruciating pain filled my stomach like a thousand hot spikes had been plunged into my flesh. I cried out in pain and hunched over, my fingers pushing into the soft skin and pressing against the firm muscles. It hurt so fucking much I almost passed out, but as quickly as it came it passed. There was no feeling there. I lay on the bed, curled up in my own urine for at least an hour before I could summon the energy to get up. This wasn't normal, something was doing this to me.

CHAPTER 11

I shovelled the congealed egg mixture into my mouth. It was tasteless and bland, no matter how much salt and pepper I mixed into it. The toast was burnt and the whole meal perfectly reflected my attitude towards eating. I felt drained, like I wasn't myself at all. The dreams I'd been having were progressively getting worse and I wasn't sure how much more I could take. I hadn't slept properly all week and it was beginning to show. My eye's were dark, my head ached and I had no interest in anything at all.

Miss Meadwell busied herself around the breakfast room, wiping down the cupboard tops and washing a number of plates that looked clean enough to begin with. Even the anger I held towards her had leaked out of me and now I felt complete numbness towards her. The only thing that annoyed me about her was that she was wearing odd stockings, one plain and the other fish net. She trotted over to wipe the plastic tablecloth from the non existent mess I had made from the meal I had barely touched. As she wiped I noticed she had a grin stretched across her painted red lips.

"You know, it's nice having a young girl around the house for once," she said smiling, obviously full of joy. Why the fuck would she care if there was a young girl around the house. "It's as though you've breathed new life into the dreary old place.

"Well I don't think much has changed. I think it's weird how you lot are always so busy and the house still looks like a hole. Why don't you guys hire more staff?" I asked, not really caring about being polite.

She looked at me a little shocked, the circular motion of her wiping slowing. She looked like a lost little rabbit caught in the headlights just before its head gets caved in by the bumper of a speeding car.

"W-well, we do try our best," she stuttered, picking up the pace with her cleaning and moving away from the table. "There's a lot to do and we don't have, well, I mean, there's no, there's always a lot to do, but the weather is lovely today isn't it?" She came back to the table, picking up my half empty plate and glass of warm orange juice. "Are you quite full? Would you like anything else to eat?"

I stared at the back of her as she carried the crockery over to the sink. What kind of answer was that? She always seemed so uncomfortable around me when I thought about it. She'd never really started a conversation like she had done today, I thought I'd take advantage of that.

"No, I'm fine thanks. But there was something I wanted to ask, what's behind the red door on the third floor?"

Miss Meadwell became silent, her cleaning stopped as she stood at the sink, not turning to look at me. It was awkwardly quiet for almost a full minute until she started stammering ums and ahs. As if to save her though, Mr Imamu came through the back door. His heavy leather boots stomping against the tiled floor as he went over to the sink, giving me a stern look. He looked into Meadwell's face as he filled his glass with water and downed it in a few gulps.

"The red door leads to Mrs Woods bedroom," he said in his thick central african accent. "It's a private room that you don't need to worry about, but I would have thought that Tobias would have told you that already. Why the interest?"

"Just wondering," I said, hiding my trepidation when I thought about the door. "I just thought it looked cool. What's wrong with Aunt Wood's by the way, what illness does she have?"

Tobias walked in from the entrance hallway, the other two looked at him and then to the floor.

"She has the flu, I thought I told you this already Miss Hammond," he said pompously.

"No, you hadn't," I mocked. "I've never seen the flu make somebody wheelchair bound."

"And what is it do you believe she's suffering from?"

"Well, I don't know."

"Miss Hammond, must you continue to defy me? Surely you have better things to do with you morning. And you two," He addressed Meadwell and Imamu who looked up simultaneously. "I'm sure this house wouldn't look like such a, hole was it? If you didn't stand around chit chatting instead of fulfilling the tasks I've given you."

"Yes sir," said Imamu, nodding his head. "I just came for a drink, I'll be heading out now." He slammed his glass on the side and stormed out quickly. Meadwell said nothing but robotically cleaned the empty glass and made her exit with her hands still wet.

"Now miss Hammond," he said, calmly placing his hands on the breakfast table and bending over to look me in the face with his bloodshot eyes. "Do you have any further questions?"

Why are you such a cunt? I thought, I could only imagine his reaction had I actually said it.

"No, I'm going outside," was all I said as I stood up. I made my exit but he grabbed me by the arm, his grip was strong and I struggled to pull myself free. I felt him squeeze as he looked down on me.

"Your great aunt is very ill, you would do well leaving her to recover and stop snooping around like this is some kind of Scooby Doo cartoon."

I wrenched my arm free, scowling at him as i practically ran out into the garden. I checked my arm, gently stroking the red marks he'd left upon my flesh.

CHAPTER 12

I walked down the path around the back of the house, rubbing my arm. I hated Tobias, he hadn't even thanked me for cleaning up the library and now he'd physically abused me. I couldn't wait for my mum to get back, hopefully she'd be able to convince Aunt Woods to get rid of him. I couldn't understand how such a nasty piece of work commanded such authority and I suspected he was at the centre of what was happening to me. I didn't know how or why, but I felt extremely unnerved when I'm around him and I just didn't trust him.

As I rounded the corner I noticed Mr Imamu weeding out a flower bed. His gardening tools were all rusted, impossible to open and he was pulling the weeds out with his hands. I marched up to him, still furious about the whole confrontation with Tobias. He didn't bother looking up as I approached.

"Why do you let him boss you about like that?" I asked angrily.

"Excuse me?" He said, eyes still fixed on his work.

"He's a lot younger than you, he's scrawnier and as far as I can tell he does nothing except boss you and Meadwell about. Why do you let him do it?

"Little girl, it's all about respect. And I guess that's something you've still got to learn."

"I'm not a little girl, and I respect people who respect me back." How dare he say that to me. He's so spineless, willing to back chat a seventeen year old girl but not the snivelling wretch he calls boss.

"Heh, you've got some nerve I'll give you that. But you still have much to learn. You are right though, I am older than Tobias, probably older than you realise, but with age comes wisdom. You learn a lot of things when you get to my age, and one of those things is what part you play in life." He seemed to enjoy speaking in riddles, keeping me guessing. I didn't really give a fuck, it's obvious he wasn't going to give me a straight answer so why should I bother. I changed the subject.

"Where's Jonah today?"

"He ain't here."

"No shit."

"He didn't turn up today. Anything else? You can help me if you wanting to."

"There's a shed in the woods, I found it the other day and I heard someone, I heard screaming. What's in there?" He finally stopped what he was doing and turned to look at me.

"You need to be careful wandering around in the woods. There's a lot of wildlife out there, not everything is safe. The woods are huge too, they stretch for miles and it's easy to get lost. Better to stay around the gardens, they should be big enough for you."

"Noted, what about the screaming?"

"It was probably a fox, I wouldn't worry about it."

"It didn't sound like a fox."

"Have you ever heard a fox scream?"

"No."

"I have, it was probably a fox."

"Whatever." I turned a stormed away. What an impetuous bastard. One minute he's being ordered around like a low life and the next he sits there acting like he's better than me and knows everything. I don't understand why Jonah likes him so much. As I thought about him I realised how much I missed him, it seemed like he was the only normal person within fifty miles of this hell hole. Without him I didn't know what I could do with the day, I was beginning to get bored of just lying in the sun and I wanted to avoid being in the house. I felt like as long as I was outside, the building didn't affect my mind as much. I turned to look at it for some reason, looking up at the tall, lead lined windows set into the brickwork.

I looked along, some were cracked, some had their curtains drawn and then, there on the third floor I saw a woman stood in the window, looking out at me, partially hidden behind a curtain. It couldn't be, but it looked like mum. She quickly darted back behind the curtain out of sight. It couldn't be mum, my mind must be playing tricks on me, it had to be Miss Meadwell, spying on me again. Probably under orders from Tobias, making sure I'm not 'snooping'. Maybe thinking about mum all the time was making me see what I wanted to. I'd give anything for her to be here right now.

I continued walking, checking the other windows as I walked, paranoid I was being watched and scrutinised. I heard a clinking noise and my attention was turned from the empty windows to the door into the kitchen. It took me a moment to register what happened, but out trotted Miss Meadwell, carrying a tray full of glasses with ice cold water, topped with lemon, a big, stupid grin across her face.

"Would you like a drink Miss Hammond?!" She called across the grass. I shook my head, confused and gawking at her limp jawed. She continued walking over to Mr Imamu, smiling idiotically.

Impossible, if she was down here, then who was that stood in the window? Adrenaline surged through me and I felt sick. I ran in the house, not really knowing what I was doing or what I would do once I had caught the imposter who resembled my mother. I barrelled through the hallways and up the stairs onto the third floor. I had come to avoid this floor as I knew the red door lurked behind a corner I could not remember, but I had to find her.

The corridors were empty and covered in the usual layer of dust, disturbed by my movements. My footsteps sounded hollow against the wooden floor as I ran, finding the doors all closed, save for one. I tentatively opened the door, the room behind was brightly lit by four large windows. It was a huge room, but sorely neglected. Inside were many toys, old rocking horses, dolls houses, army soldiers, teddy bears, pushchairs, dolls, board games and the likes, lovingly displayed but completely forgotten. It was a playroom any child would scream and beg for, if not a little dated, but it seemed the toys had not been used in decades.

There was no sign of anyone in the room and so I began to investigate. Walking up to the window I was positive this was the room I had seen her, or the image of her, stood in the window. Could I have been imagining it again? I was no longer convinced what was real and what wasn't. I continued to inspected the items dotted around the room a little more closely.

Perched on a table were a number of photographs, black and white, faded and bleached from the sunlight. I saw a young woman, posing happily with her two children. Her hair was dark and kept up in a neat bun and she wore a very elegant, very heavy looking dress. The children, a boy and a girl, were dressed in very smart clothes, possibly from the late forties or early fifties. In another picture the woman was sat and two men stood either side. One older than the other with small round glasses and a curled moustache, the other dressed in a butler's suit with his hands behind his back. Happiness seemed to ooze from the photographs, like a well knit family or group of dearly loved friends. There were others of many different people, none of whom I recognised, not that I expected to but most were taken with the house or luscious gardens as a backdrop. When I thought about it, these were the only photographs I recalled seeing anywhere else in the house.

Something about the room unsettled me, but what unsettled me more was where the woman had disappeared to. The house was big, but surely I would have walked into her on my way here. I couldn't get the image out of my head, she could have been my mothers twin, but it made no sense. She couldn't be here, not without telling me.

"Miss Hammond!" Came the pompous voice of Tobias echoing down the corridor.

I ran out of the room towards the end of the corridor, he would probably lose his shit if he knew I was poking around up here on the third floor. He hadn't explicitly said not to, but I got the impression he didn't want me exploring much of the house by myself. He continued to shout as I made my way down the double staircase in the entrance hall, trying my best to keep out of sight until I was lower down.

"Yes yes, I'm here, what do you want?" I asked attempting to keep my composure, not showing that I'd just sprinted the span of half the house. He held forward the telephone receiver impetuously, looking down at me with scorn.

"Your mother."

I snatched the receiver from him and he skulked away. This was a strange coincidence, one I struggled to believe and tentatively raised the receiver to my ear.

"Hello? Mum? Where are you?" I said breathlessly, finally gulping in the air now Tobias was out of sight.

"Calm down dear, what on Earth is wrong?"

"Where are you right now mum?"

"I'm at the hotel dear, why? What's happening?"

Of course she is, where else would she be? I really needed some sleep, my mind was unravelling and it was making me sound crazy. The last thing I wanted to do was to worry mum

"Oh nothing, I thought I saw, well, nevermind. Are you okay?"

"Yes Bea I'm fine, but are you? You sound worried."

"No I'm fine mum, I just, This place is so boring you know? I just can't wait to see you again."

"Oh I miss you too honey. They managed to get hold of your dad, he's been detained for questioning so I should be able to come and pick you up once that's all sorted. That's why I was calling, thought I'd give you the good news" She sounded relieved.

"Mum, what's going to happen to Dad?" I asked, genuinely concerned. I wasn't around when he flipped. Mum managed to get me out of there before he could find me so all I really had were good memories with him. It seemed strange to me that such a loving, caring father could go completely nuts and turn into an abusive psycho. But I guess that's how it always happens, most people aren't born crazy.

"Only what needs to happen sweetheart," she reassured, sensing the sadness in my voice. It didn't really mean anything. It could have meant a week inside or it could have been death by firing squad but at least she was still trying to protect me.

"Okay, well, tell them to hurry up."

"I will darling, I've got to go now anyway. Love you."

"Okay, love you t-." She hung up, or the phone line broke. Either way I slammed the receiver down angrily for some reason.

I sat on the bottom step thinking about Dad, what his motives were and why he had been so adamant about taking me away. He'd broken up our family and now I'd been left alone. It seemed like everyone I had ever loved were a million miles away. I then thought about Jonah, why he hadn't turned up today. I hoped he was okay and that nothing had happened to him.

CHAPTER 13

I had gone to bed early without dinner. I felt so drained all I wanted to do was sleep, I didn't have the energy to be around others. As soon as my head hit the pillow I was out and it didn't take long for me to open them again. I was sat at the table in the kitchen like I did every morning, except this time, instead of the usual spread of burnt toast, sloppy eggs, cremated bacon and cheap sausages sat platters full of raw flesh, bowls brimming with dark, congealed blood and unidentifiable entrails were strewn across the surface.

I stood up in horror and disgust, the foul stench wrestled with my stomach, forcing bile to fill my mouth as I desperately clutched at my nose the keep the feeling at bay. The normally bright and airy room was dark and red, blood spattered on every surface and dripping from the ceiling and walls. Cruel hooks hung from underneath stainless steel cabinets and wire cages were attached to the walls, viscera and gore plastered over their surfaces.

From the dark corner, three robed figures entered the room, I took a step backwards as they lined up along the opposite side of the table, their hooded heads twitching erratically. As one they dropped their robes, revealing twisted, faceless creatures with long limbs, stretched flesh and bony hands. I screamed in terror as the warped, featureless faces looked upon me from twitching heads. I turned to flee but was confronted by a fourth, naked, quivering thing that grabbed my arms and pushed me back.

I tried to fight, pushing against my attacker but its strength surpassed my weakened state. I felt the table against my back and in another moment, the remaining three creatures had swarmed over me, each taking a limb and holding me down against the piles of meat and flesh that became my mattress. I screamed the kind of scream when you know your life is in danger and there is nothing you can do to stop the course of events. I screamed so loudly my throat felt like it was tearing and still I could not free myself.

I thrashed and I pulled, tiring my already lifeless body until I could no longer resist. The creatures hands were all over me, pulling, grasping and tearing at my clothes, ripping them from me and exposing my soft, pale flesh. I lay naked in the gore, screaming and crying, my skin slick with blood, unable to escape and not knowing what these things would do to me. The table vibrated, no, the whole room vibrated. The hooks and knives that were hung around the kitchen swung from the movement, cupboard doors banged and the creatures heads moved towards a large archway at the end of the room, beyond which only darkness lay.

I strained to lift my head, if only to catch a glimpse at what drew their attention and I knew we had been joined by another. A thick, black smoked rolled in through the doorway and seeped through the grilled vents around the room like a liquid. It moved down the walls and along the floor, encompassing everything, taking up every inch of space the room had to offer. It swirled around itself and gathered at the end of the table, twisting upwards into a column that formed the basic shape of a person. From within the swirling mass of black gas, two glowing orbs appeared, red and sinister. I had seen the eyes before, beyond the red door. The purest hatred burned within them and it filled me with dread.

The smoke darkened the room, enveloping the faceless creatures into itself and absorbing them until they were nothing but smoke themselves. It more clearly defined limbs for itself, becoming solid and tangible whilst the sinister vapour somehow still held me against the table. It formed the shape of a man, terrifyingly huge with skin as black as pitch, his broad soldiers skewered by obsidian spikes that ran down and along his back and melted into the darkness that had encompassed the room. His great, muscular arms ended it terrifying, clawed hands that grasped at the soft flesh of my breasts, tearing the skin and drawing ruby blood to the surface.

A number of what I can only describe as horns jutted out at all angles from his head, curling sidewards and backwards, framing the malicious eyes that now observed me writhing in fear and agony, a cruel, tooth filled smile spread across his dark face. His powerful form opened my legs, there was nothing I could do, compared to his strength I was like tissue paper, he could tear me into a thousand pieces if he wanted. I pleaded for help from anyone and I felt his long, slick tongue moving up my body and to my neck. My hairs stood on end as the stench of rotten breath, sulphur and burnt meat left his mouth and filled my nostrils.

He said but one word, one word in that hellish voice dragged from the deepest pit. One word that tore me from that nightmare and brought me back into the conscious world.

"Mother."

*

I screamed as I awoke, calling out for my mothers aid. The room was still dark as the morning sun peeked over the horizon. I wept and wept, lying in a pool of my own sweat, shivering from the trauma I had experienced. As I threw the cover off I found myself lying naked, my bed clothes torn and tattered around me. This was real. This wasn't in my mind any longer. My limbs ached and my wrists and ankles burned. Had that happened? Whether in this world or another I knew I had been attacked, assaulted. The dark figure that plagued my dreams had some influence on me and I felt a fear I cannot describe wash over me.

I left the bed in search of something to cover myself with, tears and mucus flowing from my face. I grabbed a box of tissues from the floor by the bed and noticed something unusual. I wiped away the tears and pulled out the book, the *Legiones Inferni,* not where I had left it. Had someone been in my room while I was sleeping? Perhaps my attacker wasn't some formless creature in my mind, it could be someone very real and very dangerous. I needed to get away, but where would I go? I was miles away from any civilisation, I didn't even know which way to walk. Jonah. His farm, we passed it on our way here, me and Mum. If I could get to him I knew he would help me.

I grabbed a bag and stuffed in what I could, what I thought I'd need, it wouldn't matter once I got to the farm. I looked at the book I had thrown on the bed another time, something seemed different, the pages were misaligned, some stuck out. I picked it up and flicked to the odd sheets. Where once pages had been torn from the book, they had been replaced, stuffed back inside messily and they detailed one creature, one whom I recognised. The artist's interpretation I could say was accurate. It was the beast I had seen in my dream, it's great black form, its burning red eyes, it’s crown of horns and a pair of huge, black wings. And above the picture was a single word. Incubus.

CHAPTER 14

I stared in disbelief at the pages before me. This terrifying demon I now knew as Incubus had been haunting my nightmares since I arrived at this place. I couldn't interpret the language but there were many images that made it clear to me what I was experiencing. Old engravings of the smoke like creature hovering over a young woman's bed, paintings of his clawed fingers piercing maidens minds whilst they slept. The horrific depictions made me sick to my stomach knowing that this was happening to me. But where had the pages come from? Maybe Miss Meadwell was on to Tobias, knew he was up to something and wanted to help me. Maybe Tobias wasn't human at all. Nothing made sense but I knew that I felt like I was being watched since we first pulled up outside the front doors.

I needed to find Jonah, explain everything to him. I felt like he could help me if he didn't think I was fucking crazy. I'm positive he would understand. He could keep me hidden at his farm, safe away from this place whilst I kept an eye out for my mums car passing by. It seemed like a stupid plan when I thought it out but it was the best I had, I couldn't remain inside these walls any longer.

I pushed open the window, it squealed loudly but I didn't care. Most nights I had to open it to let fresh air in so this wouldn't seem out of the ordinary to anyone keeping tabs on me. The drop down was further than I remembered and in the early morning light I could barely see the floor. If I jumped I knew I'd break a leg or worse. The air was still and warm, hitting me like a wall as I stepped out onto the window ledge, grabbing on to the gutter pipe that fed down the side of the house from the roof. It was dry and warm but covered in a crispy moss

I didn't know if it could support my weight but I had to risk moving down it to the next ledge, there was nothing else to hold on to. I used the crumbling plaster and unevenness of the brick wall as stepping stones, clutching on to the rusted pipe so tightly it hurt my fingers. Slowly but surely I made my way down, shaking and swearing quietly to myself. This was like a bad joke, I'd sneaked out of houses before but never due to the threat of being raped by a demon. If it weren't happening to me I could never believe it, and that was the difference.

The sun began to climb higher, peering over the treelines and lighting the way below. I knew I had to get out of sight of the house before the staff members woke up and began their daily chores. I worried about Tobias the most, what if he wasn't human? What if he had some otherworldy sense and already knew I was gone, plummeting down the stairs ready to sprint across the grass to capture me and drag me back into the nightmare. I began to run, sweating already from the morning humidity. The clouds above were dark hues of reds and purples. Red sky in the morning, shepherds warning, brilliant. It felt like a bad omen.

I ran on the grass alongside the gravel path, taking care to make as little noise as possible, throwing a cautionary glance backwards every now and again to make sure the house was still dark and those crimson eyes of terror and dread were not pursuing me. I rounded the corner behind some trees and entered the wooded road that lead towards the gates. Darkness and shadows danced before me. Every unusual shape was a threat to me, a nightmarish horror lurking behind the foliage, ready to pounce as I ran passed and yank me into the torturous depths of Hell. I shook with adrenaline and pushed myself onwards.

As the sun rose I could see more and more of my surroundings but it took me a full twenty minutes to reach the gates. The grounds of the house were a lot larger than I had realised, if I were to go missing no one would know. This was dangerous, but necessary. The further I ran the more I could feel the influence of the house slipping out of my head. My mind felt lighter, but I also felt tiredness so powerful my body pleaded for me to stop, to lie down and rest my eyes. I felt like I would throw up and my head was spinning but I pushed onwards, intent on escape.

Eventually I slowed to a brisk walk. I must have been rambling for at least an hour until I finally cleared the dense, overbearing woodlands. The familiar smell of rapeseed was carried over me from a slight breeze. It reminded me of better times as the huge yellow fields came into view and the warm rays of the sun beat down on my back as I moved away from the treeline. I felt like I was approaching safety, but still I felt vulnerable out in the open. I had to walk along the road, huge lines of hedgerows separated me and the stinking fields of crops. I realised I still had a while to go and my mouth was already dry. Stupid girl, didn't bring any water.

I walked for hours longer, dragging my feet along the dirt road kicking up clouds of dry dust that stung my eyes and intermittently caused me to cough and splutter. England wasn't that big but the thought occurred to me that I might die of dehydration out here. Salvation appeared on the horizon in the form of a large, white sign. The sign to the farm that Mum and I passed in the car. Jonah's farm. My determination renewed and I pushed forwards, licking my dry lips. It didn't take me much longer to get there and I looked up at the sign, proud of my accomplishment. The white paint had dried and cracked, it was well worn and heavily battered by the elements. The painted letters were badly faded and difficult to read. *Berrington farm*.

I looked down the overgrown dirt road that lead away from the sign and curved behind a tall row of skinny poplar trees that swayed lazily in the pitiful breeze. I felt uneasy, I had never visited a farm before but I expected there to be some signs of life. There was no noise other than the breeze through the fields. No animals, no machinery, no voices. I walked towards the trees, expecting them to conceal the farmhouse with the worried feeling stirring in my gut.

I cleared the corner and felt the blood drain from my face in shock. As I had assumed, the farmhouse sat behind the trees, hidden from view of the road to maintain a level of privacy. But where I expected to see a quaint, white cottage with small barns set beside it, there sat a black, burnt out carcass where a home once stood.

CHAPTER 15

Shredded police tape blew lazily in the breeze, attached to the rotten remnant of a wooden fence post. There were no signs of life other than the various insects buzzing around the overgrown garden, busying themselves with there miniscule tasks, oblivious to the horror which had dawned upon me. There must be a mistake, perhaps the farm was further down the road, but I didn't recall seeing another farm for miles. And the name, he had said his family owned *Berrington Farm.*

I walked over to the building, working my way through tall grasses, my feet crunching against unknown objects hidden within the weeds. I had to investigate, none of this added up and I needed to get things clear. Either I was losing my mind, or everyone I had encountered in the last two weeks had been lying to me, fabricating a world of untruths for me to live in for some reason. Was any of this real, or had I truly lost my mind.

I had always been taught not to enter ruined buildings, it was unsafe apparently. Well my life had become pretty fucking unsafe right now. I entered through the charred doorway, the scent of burnt wood, damp and fungus greeted me, a mixture of unpleasant odours that warned me away but that I chose to ignore. The interior had been completely destroyed by the blaze that had evidently happened quite a while ago as vegetation had already grown in places, reclaiming the land where the building once stood.

The furniture that once made this place a home had been turned into nothing but blackened skeletons and piles of moist ash. The walls were stripped of any paper or paint, the plaster reduced to dust or bubbled in places due to the extreme heat. As I wandered through the desolate rooms the farmhouse began to take on a more sinister feel.

Etched and painted on the walls in an oddly coloured paint, at least I hoped it was paint, were strange geometric markings and patterns. Disturbing murals resembling something you'd find in a disused factory or graveyard where the 'cool' goth kids would hang out and pretend to be Satan worshippers. The only difference was that these seemed real, practised and utilised. The strange lettering was deliberate and well formed. The triangular patterns formed complicated structures, and worse of all,

I recalled seeing these same patterns in the *Legiones Inferni* on the pages regarding Incubus.

Where the fuck was Jonah?! I was getting seriously freaked out. Was I being hunted by some demon worshipping death cult? I don't know what compelled me but I continued through the house, feeling the need to discover what had occurred here. I wandered into what I deduced must have been the kitchen due to the shape of a strange, warped pile of molten metal that sort of resembled a fridge freezer in the corner, part of the ceiling collapsed over it and half burying it in rubble. There were even more of the strange markings on the wall and floors in here and also some scraps of paper, their whiteness standing out strikingly against the dirty charred floors as if intentionally placed there.

I dusted off the filth and read what I could from the heavily damaged sheet. It was part of a newspaper, the date illegible but part of one article remained in readable condition. The headline read '*Local farmhouse burnt to the ground in horrific cult ritual*'. Perfect. This wasn't the kind of thing that happened in normal life, why was it happening to me? I had never heard of any weird cults in England, I thought it was an American thing. But I suppose these kind of things aren't exactly advertised in the local paper.

I sifted through the other papers on the floor, looking for the rest of the article that had been torn off. There was nothing except obituaries, personal ads, the odd story of carrot rot. I then noticed a door to my left. It led down into the basement, into the darkness below which the light that shone through the half demolished kitchen wall lit the stairway enough for me to see the paper trail lead downwards.

Every molecule in my body told me not to descend that wooden staircase, to leave the house and continue walking until I could flag down a passing car. In an episode of sheer stupidity I cautiously made my way downwards, my curiosity getting the better of me. I tested the sturdiness of each step before putting my entire weight on it. I'd seen enough dodgy horror films to know that the girl fell through the broken step only to have her legs mutilated by whatever horrific creature was pursuing her. But this was real life I told myself.

I spied the torn piece of paper almost at the very bottom of the soot covered steps. I made my way with no incidents, other than the sheer trepidation I felt every time a step whimpered against the weight of my foot. The room was probably the worst in the house and I guessed it may have been the source of the inferno. The ceiling had been ravaged by flames, great holes yawned into the structure above allowing sunlight to filter down, lighting most of the room but leaving corners in pitch blackness. The walls didn't look man made at all due to the damage. The bricks were cracked and blistered, strange mosses growing on them giving the impression of some kind of hellish bog. The satanic murals were in abundance here but mostly the same one had been repeated. Aside from the scorch marks I also noticed a large, dark stain in the centre, surrounding a malformed stone stump.

Turning my attention to the newspaper article I soon learned what horrors had occurred here.

*

Tragedy struck the local community when reports of the most horrific crime reported in the county reached public attention in the last week of May, 1993. The house of local farm *'Berrington Farm'* was found in flames when Dr Randolph Kotter attended expecting a house appointment with the young Amelia Berrington in regards to recent episodes of seizuring and night terrors. Upon arrival at the home of four, Dr Kotter found the homestead ablaze and promptly contacted fire services.

Once the blaze was under control, firemen and police officers were able to gain access to the building in search of the family of four who occupied the residence and were well known within the community. It became apparent that the house may have been the target of a break in by a group of unknown individuals and a number of satanic inscriptions were found around the home.

As the authorities continued their search, the remains of the family were found in the basement. Upon autopsy it was found that the parents of young Amelia, Geoffrey and Ethel Berrington, had received a number of stab wounds to the chest and had been carried down into the basement. The son, Jonah, had received a deep, lacerating injury to the neck whilst Amelia herself had been restrained against a heavy plinth that had been carried into the room for what seems to be a ritualistic sacrifice, she had unfortunately perished in the flames.

The cause of the fire seemed to have been due to the dropping of oil lamps relating to a struggle, however the events of the incident remain a mystery. It is assumed that the assailants escaped and no evidence of their whereabouts has been found. Police are warning all local communities to be vigilant and report any unusual behaviour immediately.

*

I felt sick. Physically sick. As my eyes continued to read the article I couldn't believe the black typed words laid out before me. It didn't seem real, until I looked at the photograph. The image of the Berrington family, smiling happily as they posed for a stupid Christmas photo. And there he was, wearing a goofy reindeer jumper, Jonah sat grinning, mockingly. Jonah was dead, he had died in this terrifying murder over a year ago. My Jonah, the handsome farm boy I had grown so attached to over the last two weeks.

I sat on the step as my head spun from the overwhelming information. My life had been transformed into a spiralling maelstrom of impossible events and I barely registered the creaking sound behind me. All I knew next was a sharp pain at the back of my head, a high pitched ringing in my ears and then numbing darkness as I fell into unconsciousness.

CHAPTER 16

My head felt like a heavy bag of wet sand and I strained my sore neck muscles in an attempt to raise it. My vision was fuzzy and my eyes struggled to focus on anything as I forced them open. The back of my head felt damp and pain throbbed constantly with each beat of my heart. I struggled to remember what had happened, where I was and how I got here. I remembered the basement, the newspaper, the pain and then darkness. I was sat up, uncomfortably slung forwards with my hands tightly tied behind my back with thick, rough rope. My shoulders ached almost as much as my head.

I looked around my new prison, it was dark outside and the room was small but I recognised the musty, dank scent of the horrifying house I thought I'd escaped from. Whoever had attacked me had gone through the effort of dragging my unconscious body back here, imprisoning me for some nefarious reason. My panic increased when I was able to see more clearly what surrounded me. The same ritualistic markings that had been found at the farm were painted meticulously on all of the surrounding walls. The strange red paint seemed to glow faintly in the dim light.

The room was square with only one entrance situated directly in front of me. To my right were two tall, thin windows, the drab curtains hanging lifelessly open allowing the light of the full moon to stream in. The floorboards were bare but covered in a thick layer of dust and dirt disturbed by a number of footprints and the paper that hung from the walls was peeling and torn. I had never seen this room before but I had no doubt in my mind I was back at my great aunt's house.

The door before me opened, the light from the hallway creeping around it, towards me. The lightbulb above my head buzzed into life, the filament shining brightly, illuminating the cage I had been stored in with a sickly, dim, yellow light. The door opened fully and two figures walked inside one by one. They wore dark robes but their faces were exposed. Miss Meadwell and Mr Imamu, both with a sinister grin spread on their crazed faces.

"What the fuck is this?" I asked, holding back tears and hiding the dread I contained within myself. "Why are you doing this to me?"

"I told you that you breathed new life into this house deary," said Meadwell in a creepily pleasant tone.

What the fuck was happening, what's wrong with these people. Imamu just smiled and stared like a psycho. Their hands were hidden but I imagined all kinds of brutal torture implements hidden beneath the rough material that they had fashioned into ritualistic robes. My thoughts wandered to the poor girl, Amelia, who had been found tied to a stone plinth after being burned alive in the farmhouse. Was that part of the ritual? What had they done to her before setting her alight? I thought again of Jonah, his throat slit, left to bleed to death on the dirt ground, but somehow able to converse with me, to bond with me over the past two weeks.

As I sat and contemplated about the events unfolding before me, worried about what was about to happen, a third figure skulked into the room. Tall and slender with their hood drawn up concealing their face in shadow. Tobias, the fucker, what was he trying to do, scare me? I scowled at him, the fear inside of me transforming into rage and anger. I knew it, from the moment I met him I knew he was behind all of this. He had probably been drugging me with psychoactive drugs, causing the horrid nightmares, hallucinations, memory loss. There was no demon, there was just him, leading this cult, preparing to murder me.

"You bastard, you fucking bastard. Why? Why are you doing this?!" I screamed.

"Now young lady, watch your language. I thought I taught you better than that."

My mouth dropped, I felt the blood leak from my face and my eyes widen in shock. The voice wasn't Tobias' at all. It was feminine but full of mocking hate. It was a voice that was all too familiar to me and as the figure pulled back their hood my worst fears were realised.

"Mum?"

"Hello Bumble Bea."

Was this some kind of elaborate joke?

"Mum, w-what's happening here? Mum, please," I sobbed, my brain couldn't process any of this.

She walked forward smiling and gently wiped away the crystal tears rolling down my cheek with her soft hand. The familiar and comforting scent of her perfume reminded me of my childhood, sat on her knee as she cuddled me whilst watching garbage TV and inappropriate cartoons. I felt safe then, now I only felt confusion and fear.

"Shh dear, don't worry, we've done this many times."

"Done what?" I asked, looking up at her with a worried look on my face.

"Oh there's no need to worry honey. You're going to be a mother, it's really quite an honour. If not a little painful." She smirked evilly as her sentenced ended in words I would never expect to come from my own mothers mouth.

"Praise Lord Incubus," chanted the two ghastly figures stood behind her in a chilling monotone voice.

"Mum? What the fuck do you mean?!" I screamed. Her hand moved so quickly I barely registered the movement but the sharp sting on my cheek let me know she had swiftly slapped me.

"You stupid little bitch. If you stop your screeching I'll tell you. I always love to see your faces when I tell you." She smiled menacingly. "We worship our Lord, Incubus. His is a constant cycle of death and rebirth. He must be born into this world through a mortal and when he is he grants us, his disciples eternal life and when his glorious light fades from this world, it stands to us to herald his reawakening. The time has come for him to be born anew, we attempted it before with that disgusting family of farmers down the road. Unfortunately it didn't go quite to plan, your boyfriend put up a little fight before his sacrifice and we had to abandon the ritual. Incubus was born prematurely and was forced to take refuge in the body of someone close by. Luckily, this pitiful old woman was weak enough for him to work his way inside. Unfortunately she's too old, too feeble to carry him to full term and soon her flesh will melt away into nothingness, her energy and her life spent for the greatness of our Lord.

But do not fear my sweet daughter, we always have contingencies. I had been raising the perfect host, as I had done many times before. Being my own blood, Incubus would grant me even greater gifts once his holy form walks the Earth once again."

"What do you mean many times before, you have other daughters?" I asked confused. She laughed.

"You stupid little cunt, you don't even realise how old I am. I've had many daughters and all of them have screamed in magnificent agony, offering up their bodies and souls to Incubus, to deliver him into existence. He'll be here soon, he had to weaken your mind first, to allow him to get inside you, to plant his seed within you."

I felt nauseous. Everything she was saying sounded like some sick nightmare, ripped from the script of a terrifying nightmare or torturous tome of forbidden texts. This Demon, Incubus, he was going to rape me and impregnate me with himself? And this was all orchestrated by my own mother.

"So you'll condemn your own daughters and your own aunt for your own selfish desires?" I questioned, attempting to appeal to her humanity, if she still had any. She only laughed, cackled like a whorish witch.

"That old bitch isn't my aunt. She was just in the wrong place at the wrong time. We took care of her staff members so we could live here and conduct the necessary preparations without attracting suspicion. Luckily we have members around the country to help us and keep the police following dead end leads."

As she continued to monologue, explaining the vile plans of the cult and how they came into fruition, I heard an ominous sound from outside in the hallway. A dragging, fumbling sound. The door opened and Tobias entered the room, garbed in the same, dark robes and dragging with him another person. A sack over their head concealed their identity but he was male, his hands bound, his clothes torn and bloody from the numerous gashes and wounds inflicted upon him. Imamu assisted Tobias in hauling the poor man into the corner, propping him up against the wall and Tobias drew a long, curved blade from his sleeve, gripping it in joyous glee, ready to inflict pain and misery. Mum, Judith, looked at me, recognising my panicked confusion.

"As well as a host, the ritual demands a blood sacrifice." She nodded to Tobias who quickly removed the burlap sack that was covering the strangers face. "We've had him for a while, he's been kept in the woods. Mr Imamu has made sure to keep him concealed and *comfortable.*"

"Dad?!" I cried as he sat slumped in the corner, his eyes caked in blood, his skin pale and damp with sweat as Tobias' horridly grinning face mocked me from above. It was him screaming in the woods, I was so close to him, I could have helped him but instead I ran away scared like a stupid little girl. He looked so weak, I couldn't imagine the horrors inflicted upon him at the hands of the monstrous cultist Imamu. But only too soon would I be subjected to a fate far worse. Mum walked over and pulled Dad's head up by his hair so he could see her.

"Your father discovered my true plans before he was meant to. He had found out about our group and had planned to steal you away from us before you would mature into a proper host. But he didn't try hard enough, he underestimated us, underestimated how far our influence had spread. He thought the police could help him," she laughed, mocking the poor man who winced in pain.

She had fed me lies this whole time. Our happy family life was nothing but a sick play to her. She had reared me like cattle in order to slaughter me for her blasphemous God, and it wasn't the first time she had done it. My dad was just a pawn in her insidious game and would be murdered for falling for her twisted plans. He managed to force his blood encrusted eyes open and gazed in my direction. Complete remorse filled his face when he realised I, his only daughter, had been captured by these psychotic cultists, strapped to this chair ready to be sacrificed. He wept, sobbed loudly and struggled against Tobias. Imamu strolled over and controlled Dad with a forceful jab to the face. I screamed for them to stop, screamed so loud I thought I tore my voice box.

The lights flickered and the floorboards trembled. I looked around the room and the four cultists turned towards the door. The hallway lights dimmed and heavy footprints could be heard approaching the room. It sounded like the heavy hooves of a shire horse were stomping down the old wooden floor but as I looked on, a human shape appeared in the door frame. The cultists bowed and into the dim light of the room, Jonah entered, his body naked, his skin rippling, peeling and pulsating. His eyes burned into mine like fiery red coals and I screamed in terror.

CHAPTER 17

I screamed and thrashed in my chair against the coarse restraints that held me in place. Smoke began to fill the room from some unknown gateway hidden in space. I pulled my arms, felt the rough rope cutting into my skin. Jonah stepped forwards, his perfect, tanned skin falling away to reveal a squirming black mass underneath, leaking viscous black fluid that spat, spluttered and smoked as it hit the aged wooden floor boards.

"Your struggle is in vain child," he spoke in a voice that was not Jonah's. It was deep and terrible, causing the glass in the windows to shudder and the blood in my veins to boil. Time slowed as he spoke to me and all sound became like a distant echo. There seemed to be only me and him, his crimson eyes burning into me, his gaze hot on my skin and the smoke harsh in my lungs.

"Soon I shall discard this incorporeal form, we shall be joined body and soul and you shall experience pleasures unknown to this world. You think you have experienced pain in this life? You will long for it, beg for it. What you shall feel shall be so much more. You shall become my mate and my mother, I shall share with you my seed and shall grow inside of you before erupting in glorious ecstasy. Your soul shall be a small price to pay so that I shall walk this Earth."

He walked forward and placed a hand on my shoulder, his flesh burned mine and I screamed in pain. Those inhuman eyes remained locked on mine as he smiled, standing between my bound legs. His evil presence was overwhelming, but I felt another beside me. Invisible to me and also to him. I felt the rope that held my hands together loosen as the blood dripped from their fibres. Was this his doing? Was it a trick or a game? He knelt down before me, his long, pink, serpentine tongue slithered from his mouth and explored my face as I winced, straining my head away from him.

The next moment the room was plunged into darkness, as the light of the filament bulb failing. The room became silent and I could hear only my own breathing. In an instant the room was illuminated once more, only this time in a pure, red light, bright and overwhelming. Jonah was gone, only the figures of the cultists stood before me, looking confused and concerned. Yet we were not alone.

Judith screeched as she was taken by the corpse of a woman, her emaciated arms wrapping around Judith and bringing her to the ground. Similarly Tobias and Imamu were seized by strange wraiths who had appeared from nowhere and nothingness. The screeches of the ghostly females was terror inducing and the room erupted into chaos. My bonds fell to the floor freeing my hands and I stood ready to flee for my life as the macabre dance before me continued. As I prepared my escape, there came a sickening sound from behind me. Horrid yet familiar, a wheezing breath, a mucousy pattern of breathing and a vomit inducing stench of rotten flesh. I turned and saw the corpse stood, tall and impossibly thin, her dead, milky eyes looking down at me sorrowful, her lipless mouth drooling as the wet hair that hung from her scalp was caught and matted between her teeth.

I stood frozen in terror, staring at the the creature from my dream, one who had plagued me from a child, her face burned in my memory. She stood motionless as chaos reigned around us and then she spoke, her wet voice bubbling from the mess that was her mouth.

"Kill her, save us."

In that instant the red light faded, replaced by the dim orange of the filament bulb. The strange creatures had disappeared and the cultists were left squirming on the floor, fighting nothingness as confusion swept over their faces, screaming at non-existent horrors. Dad seized the opportunity, darting forwards to grasp the curved blade from the floor and pushed it into the body of Tobias as he lay on the floor.

"Run Bea!" He shouted, looking up at me with the face of a man who had already accepted his own death. Hearing his voice for the first tie in over a year caused me to want to stay, I wanted to help him. After I willingly abandoned him he was still willing to risk his own life in order to save mine. I knew if I stayed we would both be dead. Unwillingly I ran for the door as Judith screamed for someone to grab me, that the ritual was at risk.

I flew down the corridor, passing horrid red markings etched into the walls. Crashing footsteps to my rear alerted me to the fact that someone was giving chase. I dared not turn to see who it was and instead hurtled towards the entrance hall. I flew down the steps two at a time, my legs weak and sore but the adrenaline fuelling my escape. I knew I could not run forever, I needed to hide or fight back. I turned a corner and headed for the kitchen.

The room was dark but the moonlight reflected from the silver shafts of kitchen knives stored in a block on the counter. I pulled one free, turning to face my pursuer as she entered through the door, breathing heavily after the chase.

"My, I'm surprised you still have the energy to run so fast Bumble Bea," she said mockingly.

"Shut up! Don't call me that!" I choked through the tears. My hands were shaking as I pointed the blade towards her. "Did you ever even love me?"

"Of course I did," she laughed. "You were very important to me, to all of us."

That was it, the answer I had expected. She hadn't loved me, not as a daughter. Only as a tool, a vessel to be used and cast away until the next one would be necessary. It sickened me to think how many times this cycle had been repeated, not only with Judith's daughters, but with other innocents like the Berrington family. I needed to stop this, but how, I couldn't kill Jonah and killing Judith wouldn't stop anything if what she had been saying was true of the cult. What had that spectre meant?

Judith lunged forwards, I thrust the knife into her but succeeded only in piercing her robe. We fell to the floor, the knife tumbled from my hands and hers wrapped around my neck viciously with murderous intent. Her grip tightened and I gasped, my fingers desperately trying to prize hers from around my windpipe. I looked up to see burning red eyes staring down at us and the malevolent voice of Incubus filled the room.

"Yes my child, subdue her so that I may be released of this pitiful confinement. The spirits of the damned shall not halt your holy actions again."

Judith looked up in joyous ecstasy at the praise of her lord. My vision blurred as my brain was starved of oxygen. My body began to spasm and my arms fell to the side becoming numb but able to sense the cool metal of an object lying closely to my hand. I forced my fingers to tighten around its shaft as Judith cackled in glee. With what remaining strength I had left, I blindly brought my arm up rapidly and with terrible force.

Something warm hit my face and dribbled into my mouth. I felt the grip around my neck loosen and greedily gulped down fresh air. Judith looked down at me, her eyes wide and her mouth open in disbelief. Her hands moved to her neck and over the long handle of the knife that jutted out from the pouring gash in her windpipe. She fell, rolling onto her back as her body twitched and dark blood spurted from her mouth.

"No," she gasped. "No, no, this cannot b-be. I-I have lived too l-long. H-help m-me."

I stood, rubbing the bruised flesh around my neck, coughing, my eyes stinging. I looked at her, she looked back at me. I saw fear in her eyes, real fear as a dark pool of blood began to grow from beneath her. I had never seen anything die in front of me before, and as I looked down at her pitiful body, I felt only anger and rage. She wasn't my mother and she never had been.

"Fuck you."

CHAPTER 18

I knelt down next to Judith's now lifeless corpse, her blank eyes staring up into nothingness as a trail of crimson ichor flowed from her mouth. I yanked the kitchen blade from her neck in a spattering burst of gore. Oddly, I felt emotionless at the fact I had just murdered my own mother. In fact if I had to say that I felt anything I'd have to admit ashamedly that I felt satisfaction. Abruptly I was overwhelmed by a terrible pain, searing hot pain that burned behind my eyes like my skull had been cracked open and filled with boiling water. I fell to the ground grasping my head.

"Foolish child, you cannot resist me," came the demonic voice of Incubus.

From the floor I looked up and saw the half body of Jonah, wreathe in black mist staring down at me, his face emotionless and neutral as barely any skin clung to it.

"I'll kill you like I killed her!" I shouted in defiance. In truth I was petrified, this inhuman being permeated vileness and my body wanted to flee but couldn't.

"She was weak, she was nothing. You cannot kill me, I know not what it is to die. I am eternal, I am born of darkness and in the absence of light I live on."

His voice filled me with despair, he spoke to me from millennia passed, from the darkest reaches of the abyss. With every ounce of energy I thrust the knife upwards and into his abdomen, but all the force I applied sailed through him and I fell forwards. His form was not physical in any sense other than his image, I had caused no damage because he was not there and he ridiculed me as I hit the floor, smashing my chin against the tiles causing blood to ooze between my teeth. How could I defeat what isn't there? And then it hit me, he did exist, he had a physical form, it just wasn't here. I've known where he was all along, his wickedness poisoning this house like a tumour. I had been shown, in my dreams. The horrific corpses of those women, they'd been helping me, warning me. Perhaps they had been his former victims, cursed, damned souls fighting back against their demonic master.

I pushed myself up, clutching the knife in my bruised and bloodied hand. I could kill him if I could make it upstairs, I didn't know what power he possessed, whether he could hurt me or not. Whilst I was bound I could feel his touch, he moved my legs, he must have some influence in the physical world.

I bolted for the kitchen door, his black hand reached out and grabbed me by the hair, pulling my head backwards. I let loose a guttural scream as I swung the knife wildly behind me, feeling my hair drop as the knife passed through his arm, a trail of dark mist following behind. Free I ran, as fast as my aching legs would take me, back up the stairs, upwards towards the nest of evil above.

I heard a scream echoing through the hallways, the same scream I had heard in the forest. Dad, what was happening to him? I had left him alone with the other cultists. What were they doing to him? As the screaming stopped the cruel voice of the beast tore through my head.

"Both of your parents lie dead, their pitiful, worthless lives at an end. But your life doesn't have to be. Relinquish yourself to me and be at peace knowing that you shall birth greatness," He chimed as I limped onwards, trying to block his words from my mind. "Beatrice!"

The floorboards shuddered and the walls cracked as foul energy pulsed through the house. From the cracks a thick, black liquid began to pour, like oil or tar. The smell of burning timber drifted through the air and another violent quake threw me against the balustrade of the first floor gallery. As my ribs hit the mahogany handrail I looked down into the entrance hall. The entire floor was a swirling pool of black smoke, twisting and creeping with purpose. Escape was impossible, I had to end this.

I continued on, upwards to the uppermost floor and down the twisting, narrow corridors. I normally avoided this floor and so had no idea where I was going. Left, right, left, it was like a maze of tight, dark hallways. I feared that somebody would leap out of one of the many doorways and kept the knife pointed forwards. Where the fuck was I going?

"This way."

That quiet, whispering voice, I had heard it before. She lead me to the red door in my dream. I cautiously ran in the direction I thought It came from.

"Beatrice, where are you going? What do you think you can accomplish?" Chided the incorporeal creature from nightmare realms, his unseen presence digging my every move. The walls had become disgusting, fleshy, writhing surfaces of putrid gore as I approached my goal, bleeding and oozing foul smelling liquid. I saw the turn that would lead me to the foot of the stairs, the red door awaiting me. I ran up them and grabbed the black, iron handle. My skin whistled as the hot metal burned my flesh. I screamed in pain, dropping the knife and clutching my hand as it instantly blistered. I pushed against the door with my shoulder but it was useless. I was too weak, too painful. I slid down the wall, squatting against the floor as tears erupted from my pained eyes, rolling down my face. There was nothing more I could do. I felt numb in the face of what was to come, I could hear the footsteps approaching from down the corridor.

Soon Incubus would take me, violently and painfully. He would gestate inside of me until he was ready to emerge in blood and gore, ready to unleash evil upon the world in a manner I could not fathom. I was only one in a long line of victims and soon I would share in their misery. I closed my eyes, I didn't want to see it.

"Bumble Bea?"

"Dad?" My eyes opened, I looked down and saw him, bloodied, wounded, but still him, still my dad. "Dad! How did you escape?!" I flung myself down the steps as he plodded up them. He winced in pain as I threw my arms around him.

"It wasn't easy, but after being locked in a shed for two weeks I got pretty used at seeing in the dark. Those guys, weren't so tough." Even now he was trying to be light hearted, while blood oozed from lacerations and slashes in his skin. His eye was swollen and purple, his lip split in two places. He was a mess. "Come on Bea, we need to get out of this place. I don't know what's happening but this whole house is fucked up and there could be more of them out there."

"Dad I'm sorry, I shouldn't have left with Mum, I shouldn't have believed her." I couldn't control myself, I was babbling and sobbing. I was simultaneously ecstatic to see him and ashamed. I felt like I had betrayed him, left him alone twice and yet he still came back for me.

"Oh Bea I'm sorry too. I tried to find you, tried to get you away from her. We were both fooled by her. You don't need to apologise." He cradled me like he used to when I had nightmares as a child, stroking my now greasy hair. How could I have ever doubted the love that he had for me. "Now come on, we have to move."

"No, Dad. We have to stop him,"I said, gesturing towards the door. He looked confused, pulling my arm, wanting me to leave with him. "Behind there is the source of all this. We kill it, it all stops." Of course that's what I assumed, I knew about as much of what was happening as he did, but he understood.

He pushed me to one side and with all his remaining strength forced his shoulder into the door. The wood splintered and the frame cracked as the door swung open. Dad fell into the room and rolled along the floor into the darkness. The house shook violently again, the beasts sanctum had been breached. I picked up the knife from the steps and followed him in.

CHAPTER 19

The room stank of rotten flesh and shit. I gagged as the hot air hit me and the putrid bodies of huge black flies hit my face. I swallowed down the contents of my stomach and moved over to my dad slumped on the ground. I placed a hand on his shoulder and slowly he pushed himself up on shaking arms, assuring me he was fine.

“P-Please...” Came the weak, breathless voice of a woman, concelead by the mirk and gloom of the shadowy room. We turned in unison to witness the horror of what lay before us. At the end of the room was an old, wooden bed frame. Atop the soiled, bloodied mattress lay the emaciated, skeletal form of Mrs Woods, only her abdomen was huge, much larger than that of an ordinary pregnancy, stretching the pale skin to its limits as dark, veins snaked over the skin, pulsating and throbbing. It writhed and squirmed from the evil life that was contained within. Mrs Woods clutched the brown bed sheets with her blood encrusted hands, her fingernails bending and snapping as waves of pain swept through her ruined form.

Dad stood up in horror and moved as if to run to her side in aid but in retaliation he was instantly thrown backwards as a great pillar of smoke flowed from underneath the bed, engulfing him and slamming him up against the wall. I could only scream and watch in terror. The vile plume of colourless gas emerged from the bed in a huge mass, forming in front of me as its surface constantly moving, twisting and changing until eventually it formed into a solid form.

He stood towering over me, his head was crowned in countless black horns that curled around and outwards viciously. His glowing red eyes looked on me with pure contempt and drool seeped from his pointed, bestial teeth, a mocking grin illuminated in the darkness of his face. Four tense, muscular arms hung by the side of his pure, black body and two bat like wings spread out behind him almost endlessly like the void of the abyss. Within the darkness of those dreaded wings I saw hopelessness. He grabbed me by the throat and lifted me off of the ground. I clasped the rough, boiling flesh of his arm in retaliation. His grip was like iron and I struggled to breath. He brought me close to his face. His breath was like sulphur and his jaw opened, revealing the fires of Hell that burned inside of him. His long, snake like tongue slithered out and licked up my neck and down my top. I felt it slither between my breasts and down my navel as he violated me with the moist rope of flesh.

I hung there gasping for air and with his remaining limbs he tore the clothes from my body, swiftly and painfully. I wriggled and thrashed in the air naked until he threw me to the ground with a loud crack as the bone in my arm shattered against the floorboards. I cried out in pain and he stepped forwards.

"You will not enjoy this child. But you should be filled with honour at what you are about to receive," he said, his voice so clear in my head as everything else became a blur.

He dropped to the floor and bounded over to me, his great, black form moving on top of me. With one pair of arms he held my arms up and with the other he parted my legs.

"*They* cannot save you this time," he taunted. His eyes stared into mine as he panted with anticipation, burning into my soul and then he screamed. A scream of inconceivable pain. I felt hot liquid spill over my body and he recoiled backwards, holding on to his abdomen. Thick blood poured from a wound that had materialised in his flesh. He looked towards the bed, as did I.

The mattress was empty, save the foetid stains that had been left there. Mrs woods lay on the floor, propped against the end of the bed frame and in the dim light I saw a flash of light reflect from something metallic. The knife I had kept with me, I had dropped when Incubus seized me, it had now found a place jammed into the bulbous abdomen of the frail old woman, her shaking hand wiggling it in her own abdomen as her face contorted in pain.

The beast cried out in agony and the smoke that held up my dad dematerialised, dropping him to the floor. The creature convulsed and dragged himself towards the old woman who began to repeatedly stab the knife into her wretched belly, blood gushing from the wounds as she wept. Incubus' form began to loose shape as he crawled, the hard skin melting into a viscous slop that spread across the floorboards, leaking into the cavity below until he eventually collapsed, dissolving into nothing but a dark, putrid stain.

After a moment it was over. The violently shaking house became still. The terrifying noises from below quietened, the smell of fire and ash dissipated and the demonic threat disappeared. I lay on the floor naked and traumatised. I pulled myself over to the bloodied, wheezing form of Mrs Woods, her eyes rolling in their sockets as the life began to fade from her. I gently clasped her skeletal hand and looked into her eyes.

"Thank you," was all I could say. She was innocent in all of this, a victim of horrific circumstance but still had the courage to do what was needed. She smiled up at me and her eyes closed for a final time. She breathed deeply before her chest stopped moving and she slipped into eternal slumber. I closed my eyes exhausted. Sharp pains shot up my broken arm but I could not stay awake. My head was as heavy as a stone slab as the trauma finally caught up with me. My body shut down and I fell into the familiar darkness of unconsciousness.

*

The place I was in was darker than I ever could imagine. The complete lack of light was difficult to process and strange, unformed images floated across my eyes. I was hot, sweating as I groped around, trying to find a clue as to where I was. The ground was hard and rough like stone, but warm to the touch. There was a constant noise, quiet at first and I stopped to listen. They were screams, screams of thousand of people, crying out in pain and anger. The screams became louder and louder, drumming in my mind, tearing through my ears like the screech of violins. I pressed my hands to my ears and knelt on the ground.

I felt a hand on my shoulder and turned around, startled. There was light from some unknown source, illuminating the woman stood before me. Her hair long and dark trailing over her shoulders and framing her beautiful face. She smiled at me affectionately, a warm smile that filled me with hope. A moment later she embraced me, hugging me tightly. I didn't know her but I reciprocated and a strange emotion flooded through me. I felt the most sincerest of love and gratitude though not a word was spoken. We held each other tightly and cried for what seemed like an eternity, I felt like I had known her my entire life but at the same time she was like a stranger in a crowd.

Eventually she let go, stepping backwards, the gentle smile spread across her warm face.

"Who are you? Where am I?" I asked. She didn't reply, gently shaking her head and remaining silent as she moved further away from me. I Wanted to follow her but I found that my feet wouldn't move. She began to weep and her face turned from one of warmth and love to one of utter despair and fear. In an instant her body was engulfed in flames that erupted from a gaping maw in the ground. Her flesh boiled and her body blackened until she was completely obliterated, rendered into ash. The flames spurted violently around me, burning fiercely but not lighting the shadows which encompassed me. The many screams intensified and a terrifying, demonic howl erupted from the gaping, flaming gateways.

CHAPTER 20

I blinked my eyes open, rubbing them with my sore hands as the bright sunlight blinded me. I felt a little nauseous and it became apparent that I was moving. I sat up to see rows of yellow rape flying past in a blur. Dad was in the driver's seat and I was lay in the back, wearing his shirt and covered by a thin blanket. The window was open and cool air flooded the car, blowing my hair over my face. I was a mess, my neck was badly bruised and my arm was on fire, wrapped tightly in torn material with something hard and rigid bandaged in as a makeshift splint. I could feel my fingers throbbing and attempted to move them to make sure I didn't have any nerve damage or anything.

As painful as I was I could only smile. Dad didn't know that I was awake but the sight of him speeding down the road, desperate to get us away from that house filled me with joy. To think that this nightmare could have been avoided if I hadn't have listened to mum, Judith, and just followed my gut. As I moved he turned to look at me and smiled.

"Oh Bea, you're awake," he said grinning, his face severely bruised and red, with a deep gash in his forehead but the expression of relief and love explicitly evident.

"Dad you look terrible."

"Don't worry about me. We need to get you to a hospital. I don't have a clue where we are but it's pretty much impossible to get lost these days. Do you think you'll be able to hang on?"

"After everything that's happened, I'm pretty sure I could survive a car journey with you."

We both laughed. I flung my arms around him and he held on to my forearm. Maybe we didn't need anyone else to be happy. We could do it alone. He was all I needed. But it was probably not going to be so easy. As we hugged each other, not paying any real attention to the road, neither of us saw the figure in black stood in the centre, nor did we see the foreboding glisten of the metal strung across the road like cruel, sparkling stars, their pointed tips sharp and eager.

Printed in Great Britain
by Amazon